The Whites of Gold

Samuel Lock has worked as a painter and stage designer, and as a scriptwriter in the documentary cinema. He is the author of five plays and two previous novels, including *As Luck Would Have It*, which won the Sagittarius Award in 1996.

by the same author

AS LUCK WOULD HAVE IT
NOTHING BUT THE TRUTH

Samuel Lock

The Whites of Gold

JONATHAN CAPE
LONDON

Published by Jonathan Cape 2001

2 4 6 8 10 9 7 5 3 1

Copyright © Samuel Lock 2001

First published in Great Britain in 2001 by
Jonathan Cape
Random House, 20 Vauxhall Bridge Road,
London SW1V 2SA

Random House Australia (Pty) Limited
20 Alfred Street, Milsons Point, Sydney,
New South Wales 2061, Australia

Random House New Zealand Limited
18 Poland Road, Glenfield,
Auckland 10, New Zealand

Random House (Pty) Limited
Endulini, 5A Jubilee Road, Parktown 2193, South Africa

The Random House Group Limited Reg. No. 954009
www.randomhouse.co.uk

A CIP catalogue record for this book
is available from the British Library

ISBN 0–224–06120–8

Papers used by Random House are natural,
recyclable products made from wood grown in sustainable forests;
the manufacturing processes conform to the environmental
regulations of the country of origin

Typeset by Palimpsest Book Production Limited,
Polmont, Stirlingshire

Printed and bound in Great Britain by
Biddles Ltd, Guildford & King's Lynn

for
Alan Hollinghurst

Observe yourself carefully. Of all the feelings you have ever had, has a single one disappeared? No – every one of them is preserved, is it not? Every one. The memories in one's heart never fall into dust, and when you peer down the shaft they are there below; looking up at you with their open unmoving eyes.

Gustave Flaubert

FOREWORD

THE MATERIAL FOR this book has been provided by an autobiographical piece of writing that came into my possession a long time ago – now almost ten years. It was given to me by someone I had then known for about eighteen months, the manageress of a small, bistro-style restaurant in South Kensington, where I had first been taken by friends who told me they liked the place a lot. Mostly, they said, because of Thelma, the manageress, who obviously enjoyed what she was doing and made her customers feel so welcome. Also, they said, because the food, though simple, was good, and reasonably priced as well; and because the people who ate there were usually rather interesting.

All of which proved to be true; and which is why, after that initial visit, it quickly became a favourite eating place of mine; particularly if I was alone, when I knew that Thelma would greet me warmly and be attentive, finding a table for me in a corner where I could read or sometimes, when the need was pressing, even do a little work – a little writing, that is.

Then one evening, as I sat scribbling away after supper, Thelma came up to me and asked if I was a writer: to which I answered yes, since it was pretty obvious from what I was doing that I was.

'Have you always been one?' she enquired.

'Not always,' I replied, 'but for some time, though.'

'Fascinating,' she said with a generous smile, and moved away, showing me that she didn't want me to think her too inquisitive. After that, I would often take a notepad with me when I went there to eat, or perhaps a few pages of something I had already written but with which I was not yet pleased.

Then – this must have been about six months later, as I recall – Thelma suddenly asked if she could have a word with me – about something particular, she said – which naturally intrigued me, since she had always maintained a distance between us, as she did with all her customers.

'It's about this,' she said, as she placed a brown paper parcel on the table in front of me. 'It's a kind of journal – written by a friend of mine who has died . . . He left it to me,' she added; then went on to explain that she had been wondering what to do with it, since its contents seemed rather unusual; and she thought that with my being a writer it might possibly interest me; and might even be something I could use.

In this way, through this very slight relationship with Thelma, the material for this book came into my hands. For on reading through what she had given me, I saw that the subject matter it contained might one day reach a wider audience; which I now hope that it will.

Parts of the manuscript were written in a rather hasty, slapdash manner and the handwriting wasn't always easy to read; but much of it had been written with care and in great detail; and with a certain neatness of expression as well; so that there were moments when I began to wish that I had been the author of it myself!

Regarding the text that follows: I have had to re-work sections of it that the author left unpolished; and in order to fill out the narrative at times I have had to invent a few passages as well; which has meant that the style of the writing has perhaps become a little similar to my own. At first I believed that I would also need to re-shape the story the text has to tell, in order to give its seemingly irrational, haphazard sequences a more structured form of chronology. But in my attempts to do this, I learned that the book would quickly be spoiled, and that what the narrator sets down always springs from an inner, emotional centre to which he constantly returns; which in itself I think justifies the book's general shape and pattern.

It seems sad to think that Thelma's friend was already dead when she put the manuscript into my hands, for it would have meant much to me if I could have met him. However, although it is suppressed at moments by my own, his voice is to be heard here in these pages, and my hope is that through them he will live on; and that the story he has to relate will continue to do so as well. Whatever, I feel proud to have been made the recipient of such a gift; and by someone who appears at times in the book's narrative, by the way, but whose real name I haven't used at her request. Thelma Rillington is an invented name; as, for that matter, are the name of the book's narrator − Edwin, or 'Eddie', Carpenter − and the names of most of the book's other characters as well.

In my view, truthfulness and sincerity are what count in writing; and it seems to me that in this young narrator's story (for he was just thirty-three years old when he was working on his text) there is a fair supply of both.

Attached to the manuscript was a brief letter addressed to Thelma, which, with her permission, I have decided to use as a kind of frontispiece − partly to help lead one into the main text, and also because it offers a speedy snapshot, as it were, of the relationship that existed between Thelma and her friend.

S.L.
London 2001

Dearest Thelma,

You know just as well as I do how gravely ill I am and that I am unlikely to be here much longer – so I thought that I would add this to the things I am leaving you in my will. It is something I wrote when we were younger; out of a desire to clear my mind, I suppose, and to have set down somewhere upon paper a few of my little secrets.

You've always said that you wanted to know more about me – so now you can! I just hope that my revelations won't come as too much of a surprise, or too big a shock; but you've been my best friend for so long that I thought that you, at least, should be given the chance of gaining a fuller picture. Once you've read the stuff – if you can get through it all, that is! – just throw it away.

We've had some really lovely times together; and you and Len have always been so kind and generous towards me, which I've appreciated a lot. What you will do with all the things in my flat (that I have left you in my will, I mean) I can't think; for once you have read through what I say here, I am sure you will view them differently – or quite a few of them at least.

I've been a disturbed soul and in a way, perhaps, not a very nice one. But we are what we are – aren't we? And none of us is perfect, as they say.

Be happy, Thelma, and think of me when you can. I am sure that once I am in the Great Hereafter, the thoughts of friends will count a lot to me as they fly upwards through the ether.

With so much love to you; and to Len as well – that dear, sweet, lovely husband of yours.

Yours *ever*,
Edwin.

P.S. I would have liked to have left some of my things to Mark, since, apart from Len and yourself, he is the only person I have ever cared for – cared for deeply, that is. But I am out of touch with him now, as you know, and don't have his address: which means that he exists only in memory – as, it seems, do so many things.

THE JOURNAL OF
EDWIN CARPENTER

I

IT IS 1969 AND I am writing this in the basement flat in which I live in London. Quite why I am writing it, I don't know. It could be because I have reached a moment in my life when I need to look back, and to relate for a while to the past. Perhaps too, because it is only by writing things down that I can hope to make some sense of my life, and of the mixed-up muddle it is in my mind.

But where to begin? I dislike writing – autobiographical writing – that begins with I was born on such and such a date, and then gives the exact place of birth, the town, city, county and so forth. It would be better, I think, if I began at some point, some specific moment, that holds a particular meaning for me – one that is fixed in time by an emotion that is attached to it – then have the story spread and grow from there.

One of the strongest memories of my early years, and one that might easily be used as a beginning, is of how very nervous I felt, yet excited at the same time, when I finally took the decision to leave my father's house and so rid myself of his tyranny. I know that is a strong word to have used, but it is more than warranted, I believe, by the negative effect my father had upon me when I was small.

When I say my father's house, that sounds as if my mother had died or wasn't there, when in fact she was. It is just that she spent such a lot of her time in her room, reading or saying her prayers; and not going out very much, except to do a little shopping, perhaps, in the afternoon; and always to church on Sundays twice: at eleven o'clock in the morning, and at six in the evening for evensong, when her slightly shrill, reedy voice could be heard above the richer sounds made by the rest of the congregation and the choir.

My father rarely went with her, church being for him only on high days and holidays, as he spoke of them – meaning Easter Sunday and Christmas Day and days such as those. And always on Armistice Day, or Poppy Day as we called it; when, being an alderman of the borough, he saw it as a duty of his to attend the service held at our church in honour of those who had died in the two world wars; in the first of which he had served as a soldier himself, and had suffered the shrapnel wound that had damaged his knee, and that caused him to walk at times with a stick.

I can see him clearly. Tall, already grey-headed – and distinguished in a way; and certainly a very respected and respectable man, what one might call a real pillar of the community. But everyone who knew him knew as I knew only too well that there was something strange about his make-up: something cold, detached, that set him aside, and that made him seem different from the other local men of his age, the townspeople and various farmers of the area that he counted as his friends.

The house we lived in was quite large. It had six bedrooms (three of which were seldom used) and a spacious sitting room (it was never referred to as the drawing room) that was seldom used as well – partly because we entertained so very little, and also because of it not being on the ground floor of the house where the large dining room and the kitchens were placed; and where, at the very back of the building, there was my father's office-cum-study.

I suppose that, in a certain way, there was something Whistlerian about my father, in the sense that he might have been painted by Whistler, or indeed might have stepped out of a picture by that artist, since the tones and colours of his skin and hair tended to smudge and fuse into one, offset by the crisp whiteness of the stiff collars he put on each morning before breakfast, and kept on throughout the day. Which meant that he always had a kind of well-cut look about him, even when wearing a cardigan, which he was inclined to do indoors, and not only in the neatly buttoned-up suits he wore whenever he stepped out into the street – to walk in the town, perhaps, or to go to the Castle Inn for a drink, or on Thursdays down to the cattle market, which was close to the town's small railway station, and just a little over a mile away.

It was an often joyless life for me – particularly when I was small. With no brothers or sisters to keep me company, and with just one uncle and aunt – my mother's sister and her husband – with whom I used to spend a week or so in the summer, my early childhood days were passed in and around this house – which backed on to the churchyard, and from the landing windows of which I could see the tall, gloomy yew trees that lined the churchyard's pathways and, above them, the sturdy column of the church tower that rose swiftly into the sky. Or rose against it, rather, since my memory is of seeing its rough-faced stonework in so many different hues and colours: dull pink when the skies were grey; paler and more golden when they were bright and blue; and in winter, when everything, even the sky, seemed to be white, almost no colour at all – merely a shape, a shadow, breaking through the mists, or seeming to dissolve and then to re-form itself as the heavens released their so often heavy falls of snow and the flakes flew swiftly down, flapping savagely against the window-panes and interrupting one's vision.

That was then, however, and now is now, so many years later. Yet I can remember it all so vividly; particularly one very emotional moment when (at the age of just fifteen I think it was) I finally made up my mind that I would leave, and that, unlike the boys of the town with whom I grew up, I would reject rather than cling to the bonds and ties of family life and set out upon the adventure of making a new life on my own.

To reach the decision had not been easy. For weeks I had fretted about it, knowing the effect it would have on my parents. But as I approached my sixteenth birthday I realised that a plan had formed in my mind. Then − this was just a few months later, as I recall − I suddenly found myself in the stages of enacting it. First, by deciding on a suitable suitcase to use (we didn't have grips or holdalls in those days) − one that would be large enough to contain the various things I thought I would need. Then, by hiding this suitcase in my wardrobe, beneath a tumble of winter sweaters. Then by gradually storing up money in it; part of which I had saved out of my pocket money, and the rest I had 'borrowed' from my mother, who, whenever she asked me to buy things for her in the town, never bothered to count the change.

It was the act of gradually filling this suitcase that finally brought my project to a head, and helped me to take the difficult action I had pictured for so long. For, once the suitcase was full, and there was no further object or article of clothing that I imagined I might need, I knew that I was about to do what I so feared doing; and that on a night not far ahead − perhaps when my parents were asleep and the house and the town quiet − I would release myself from what I thought of as my prison. And by some means then quite unknown to me I would make my way to London − where, I imagined mistakenly, I would dissolve into its crowds; and, as far as my childhood home life and my parents were concerned, be lost to them for ever.

★   ★   ★

Reflecting upon it now, I cannot help wondering why it was that not just my father but that both my parents were so distant and unemotional. Had both of them suffered some form of unusual mental damage when they were young? Or was it something they had inherited? I never knew my grandparents on my father's side, because he was quite a lot older than my mother and his parents had died before I was born. But I did know my mother's parents, and my memory of them is of two cheerful country people, who, on the rare occasions when I went to stay with them, or on the even rarer ones (I can recall just two) when they came to stay with us, always startled me by the effusiveness of the quick hugs and kisses that they instantly showered upon me, and that to a certain extent embarrassed me, and made me unable to respond.

My mother hardly ever hugged me or kissed me, indeed never comforted me in any physical way, not even when she came to say goodnight. A pat on the head was the most she could muster, accompanied by a 'sleep well, dear' – said in such a tone, in such a manner, that I used to think it something she didn't quite expect me to do, because she slept so badly herself. And certainly my father never gave me a hug or a kiss. Except for the occasions when he called me into his study in order to beat me – usually for having stolen things and then hidden them (stealing was and still is quite a part of my life, I am afraid) – I cannot remember his ever having even touched me. And since he and my mother slept in separate beds and in separate rooms, I didn't think that they touched each other either.

Of course, they must have touched each other at *some* time or another, I can recall thinking when I reached puberty and my mind began to embrace the idea that for me to have come into existence my parents must have made love. But however much – even now – I try to picture it, such a conjugation seems improbable, so that at times I have the impression that I must have found my way on to this planet by some magical means or method, and that I am therefore not what one might speak of as a terrestrial human being.

Having said all that, I mustn't paint a picture of my childhood as entirely devoid of physical contact. Even if I had no brothers or sisters to romp and play with, I did have Mrs Gibson – or Amy, as I was allowed to call her – who cooked and catered for my parents, and who, with the help of one of her young cousins, cleaned and looked after the house. She was something of what one might call a rough diamond, I suppose, in that she was in no way refined in her expressions; spoke in a broad West Country accent; and sometimes – though not when my parents were around – broke wind.

'Where'ere you be let the wind go free,' she used to say to me with a laugh and then a quick kiss, as her bosom heaved up and down, and she would open a door of the big, black kitchen range, or perhaps stretch to a shelf in the kitchen's pantry. And if her young cousin happened to be there – the one who helped with the cleaning of the house – the two of them would giggle about it for quite a while; as if what most people think of as being rude was, to them, just a pleasant, humorous feature of everyday life.

I loved Mrs Gibson, and often wished that she could have lived with us in the house, so that, whenever I felt the need of it, I could have run to her for comfort. But she had a family of her own to care for and look after – Bill, her husband, and also her two sons, Tom and Paul, both of whom were a little older than myself and who used to treat me as if I were some kind of toy. By which I mean that they never called me by my name, and used to push me over whenever they felt like doing so – not in a rough or violent manner, but just playfully – and then laugh their heads off as they saw me scrambling to my feet.

We never became friends, exactly. There was always a distance between us. Perhaps, I used to think, it was because their mother worked for us, and because my father was quite a figure in the town – in that as well as being an alderman of the borough, he had at one time been a local justice of the peace – which, due to the small size of our community, I am sure must have impressed them. Yet it was through Amy's elder son, Tom, that I first learned about sex: what its purpose was; how it functioned – which, until I was almost twelve years old, had remained a total mystery to me.

I can recall how some of the older boys at school – some of the prefects, perhaps – would flick at one another with their towels when changing after a shower or after a swim: either in the school's new swimming pool, or sometimes, in summer, when they had gone for a dip in a nearby river where I would be watching them from the banks. And I had become conscious of the fact that as they were stepping out of their bathing costumes they would all be sporting erections, which they would then make jokes about and display proudly to each other; one boy having such an enormous one that he behaved in an almost lordly fashion among the rest, climbing on to a bench in the changing room, or on to one of the rocks that lined the river, to tower commandingly above them.

One day – this I remember as also being in summer, because the kitchen door was wide open and Amy was bewailing the fact that she was having to cook on the old, black range, and that the gas cooker she had been wanting had still not been installed – Tom, Amy's son, arrived at the house on his bicycle.

As soon as he came bouncing in I knew that he had come to the house with a purpose, and I quickly learned that it was bound up with the news – told to him by his mother, no doubt – that I had been given a bicycle for my birthday.

He didn't greet his mother. He just walked across the room and silently watched her kneading some dough. And she – Amy – didn't greet him, which seemed to be a habit of their family. Then Tom suddenly turned to me and said, 'Come on. We're going out. For a ride. On our bikes.'

I looked at his mother anxiously. Not because I wasn't allowed to go out, or for any reason such as that, but because I half feared that her son's sudden insistence that the two of us should go off together had perhaps made her suspicious. Suspicious of what, I didn't know. But she simply paused in what she was doing, then looked at us and said, in a very direct, simple manner, 'Be back by four the pair of you. And if you're going to the woods,' she called out after us as we left, 'don't make yourselves too mucky.'

I said nothing to this in reply – not even goodbye. I just did what I knew by instinct I had to do; which was to collect my bicycle from the shed in our backyard, then join Tom, who had already opened the yard door and was waiting for me outside.

'Come *on*!' he repeated urgently, as he sprang swiftly on to his saddle and sped away; and I did my best to imitate and to follow him.

Why had Amy thought we might be going to the woods? I often wonder. Did she know things that other people didn't know? Sometimes, when I used to look at her – moving about the house, perhaps; or pausing at one of the upstairs windows in order to clean an ear with one of her fingers (which was something she often did) – I had this sense of there being some mystery attached to her: that she was knowledgeable in some way that my parents were not; and that I wasn't either, for that matter, and perhaps will never be.

As I have indicated, the town we lived in was quite small, and was situated in the south-west corner of England – in Somerset, in fact – and close to the open spaces of Exmoor. Which meant that immediately surrounding us there were deep country lanes and twisting, turning by-roads that led off in different directions: quite a few of them to the isolated farms and villages that were dotted about the area, and some to the moors, which passed between dense clusters of fir trees lining the road at either side that had been planted for their timber. And it was in the direction of one of these that Tom led the two of us on that sunny, summer day, at times more or less standing on the pedals of his machine as the road suddenly steepened and we left the town behind us.

Eventually, and after some effort, we reached the heart of one of these densely wooded valleys, where the road had quickly transformed itself into a shaded tunnel of green. Then Tom stopped, dismounted from his bicycle, and dragged it off with him into the woods.

Knowing I was meant to do the same, I trailed with my bicycle after him as he rapidly pushed his way down a steep incline that dipped towards a small river, the thin, silvery line of which we could clearly see below us. Around us the sturdy trunks of the trees soared to a great height before bursting into the dark spread of fir that had sought and had found the light; and that now formed a vaulted canopy above us.

About halfway down this slope we came to a narrow path, just visible among the riot of moss and fern that was flourishing here and there in great patches throughout the wood. And it was towards one of these that Tom made his way, as if heading for one particular spot with which he was familiar.

We had now left the path and I noticed that the ground

beneath us was less damp; also that there was no longer any moss, only the tough, frond-shaped leaves of the wild ferns – some almost knee-high – that had now begun to envelop us, so that Tom was forced at times to push them aside to enable us to pass.

Tom hadn't looked back at me once; hadn't turned to smile or to say a word – he just pushed silently on, knowing that I was dutifully following him. Then, when we reached a very remote part of the wood, but from where we could still catch glimpses of the river, Tom threw down his bicycle, removed the light tweed jacket he was wearing, threw that also upon the ground, then quickly stretched himself out upon it with his hands clasped beneath his neck.

Again I aped his action – or aped the first part of it, at least. A little clumsily this time, I am afraid, since I allowed my bicycle to tumble away from me and to make a noisy clatter.

'Lie down,' said Tom, a little gruffly.

Again I was obedient; not quite knowing why I should be, since, although I didn't think of Tom as a friend exactly, I certainly wasn't afraid of him or in awe of him in any way.

'Close your eyes,' he said, once I was lying next to him, staring up at the vast dome of fir that arched its way above us.

'Close your *eyes*,' he repeated, raising himself on to one elbow and then leaning across to look down at me.

'Why?' I asked.

'Just do it,' he said. 'Just close your eyes.' So I did; and from the noises he made I could tell that he had returned to his former position, and that the two of us now again lay side by side, surrounded by all that greenery.

It was a strange moment for me, for I had never been alone with Tom before and I had certainly never been with any other boy to such an isolated spot in the woods. I can still hear the distant sound of the river; the occasional flutter of some small bird as it darted its way through the trees above; and the slight ticking noise of some insect that I could hear was moving close to me; when – again by the sound of his movements – I could tell that Tom had once more raised himself on to one elbow, and was looking down at me again.

I was sure that *his* eyes were open, but the spell he appeared to have cast prevented me from opening my own. And it was then that he placed one of his rough-skinned hands upon my stomach and began unbuttoning my shirt.

I kept still, thinking that that was what I was meant to do, and feeling oddly safe and secure in the belief that what Tom was doing, or what he was about to do, was in no way going to be harmful.

'Push up,' he said, as he suddenly flicked aside my unbuttoned shirt and began to pull down my trousers.

'Push your *backside* up,' he said, when he realised that I hadn't understood what he had meant. 'That's right,' he added, as I obeyed him.

'Makes it easier,' he said as he took hold of my trousers with both hands and pulled them down to below my knees, dragging my underpants with them.

And it was then that I became conscious of my having an erection; and that I was not different, as I had half feared I might be, from the boys I had seen at school. I still didn't open my eyes, but as Tom took hold of my penis and slowly began to stroke it, I was suddenly overcome by an unusual sense of pleasure. Instead of being nervous, as I was inclined to be in situations that were new, I felt quite the reverse. I didn't care where I was, or whether what Tom was doing might be right or wrong, I just felt that it was something he was meant to do: that it was something that *had* to happen; and that if Tom had not been doing it, then, at some other

13

time, and in some similar private spot, someone else – some other boy – would be doing it instead.

Tom didn't coax me to a speedy climax, much as I longed to be released. He first withdrew his hand in order to unbutton his own shirt and trousers. 'You all right?' he asked, as he pushed his slacks down over his thighs. 'Yes,' I muttered in reply, now half opening my eyes and squinting up at him and at the dark curl that had suddenly tumbled over his forehead; and he then took hold of one of my hands and drew it towards the fuzzy hair of his groin; then on to place it upon his own stiff penis, which he made us stroke together.

And so it was, and in the way I have no doubt that so many young boys first experience it, that I witnessed for the first time the quick relief of ejaculation, as Tom's body began to shudder and then began to release its sudden spurts of sticky semen.

'Now you,' Tom murmured, as he rolled swiftly on to his side; and then, within seconds, brought me to a similar point of climax.

That afternoon in the woods is fixed permanently in my mind, the memory of it bound up with time for ever. How extraordinary it is, I sometimes tell myself, that we should be blessed with such powers of recall, and be able to preserve and store so many different sounds and images. For certainly animals cannot do that. They say that an elephant never forgets, and I have read somewhere, in some book, that one particular breed of goose is known to have memory patterns that can stay with them and affect their behaviour for years. But there are no signs, it seems to me, of animals being conscious of their reflections in the way that we are able to be. When I look into the eyes of a dog, for instance, or those of a cat, I see that the past and present are more or less fused into one and that their dreamlife is in some way continuous; and it is only their desire to hunt or to play, or to simply stretch and make themselves comfortable, that guides and governs the consciousness of the hours when they are awake.

II

I SHOULD BE saying something now about my father. Having branded him a tyrant – which, although it is harsh, is none the less what he was – I wish I could be painting a fuller, more rounded picture of him. As yet, however, I cannot do that. For if I am to tell my story in a really honest fashion, then I shall need to be generous towards my father and not present him as having been simply some kind of ogre. I need to see *his* point of view, to believe that the negative effect he had upon me when I was small was not an intentional one. That he was not evil: but that he was simply lacking a certain quality of human decency; and that a concern for others – or at least for others who were close to him, such as my mother and myself – was something quite beyond him. But as I say, I cannot do that yet. The words simply aren't there. They simply aren't available. So that portrait, if I am to paint it, will have to wait.

But what I *can* write about – and what, indeed, I must – is this business of stealing, which I have mentioned twice, and which I have also said is still a part of my life. *This*, I must quickly add, is not something of which I am proud. I never speak to people about it; never boast to others about the skills I have developed over the years in the art of taking things that do not belong to me. Yet here I am in this flat, surrounded by all my spoils – or by quite a lot of them, at least. And attached to each purse, each bag, each book (I have a particular obsession regarding these), there is a memory; so that if I just look at them, or if, as I occasionally do, I handle them or touch them, the moment when I stole them then returns. Everything – the place, the time, the excitements caused by the compulsion in my mind – flies back to me out of the past, and lives again in the present.

For instance, once, on a train, I noticed a purse lying free on a seat that appeared to have tumbled accidentally out of its owner's bag or pocket. And the moment I saw it – silently, passively waiting, as if fixing itself in my mind – I knew that I would soon have to find a means of making that article mine.

This was on a train going to Salisbury, as I recall, where I was intending to spend a few days with a friend; and this too was in the summer, because although it was already late in the day, the sun had not yet set, and there were low beams of sunlight streaming in through the carriage windows. I must have been in my early twenties at the time, and the compulsion from which I suffer had not yet begun to possess me in the way that it possesses me today; but I can still sense the thrill, the excitement, the almost electric vibrations in my mind, as I worked out within seconds what I must do; and as I then rose hurriedly from my seat, and made my way along the aisle of the carriage, as if on my way to the toilet.

'I'm so sorry,' I said to an elderly gentleman, as I deliberately knocked against his shoulder.

'It's quite all right,' he replied, in a very friendly manner. He looked up at me, and I smiled graciously in return; then at the lady who sat facing him, and who, I had quickly decided, must be the owner of the purse.

'Just tripped,' I said. 'So sorry,' as I affected to regain my balance.

'It's quite all right,' the man repeated, again with a smile, and I bent quickly down in the aisle and pretended to be fixing the lace of one of my shoes.

'Is something wrong?' the lady asked.

'Not really,' I answered, with a quick grin, and with one swift movement of my hand I pushed the purse close to the seat's edge, then caused it to fall on to the floor; which neither the man nor the woman seemed to notice: the sound of it being smothered by the general rattling noise of the train, and the sight of it by the fuss that I had been making over my shoe.

I knew, for this was something I had learned, that what I must *not* do was to take the purse immediately. That I had simply to be patient and wait for the train to stop. If the purse had not been missed by then, I felt sure that the owner would leave the train without it and that the prize would become mine.

Which is exactly what happened. By chance my timing had been perfect, in that I had happened to make my way to the toilet as the train was about to arrive at Salisbury, which had helped to make my action seem a natural one. On my return, as I made my way back to my seat, I again smiled at the elderly couple, in order to divert their attention a second time, and so prevent their being able to gather themselves together before the train came to a halt. Which meant that they had to more or less scramble out of the carriage, the man having hurriedly brought their suitcases down from a luggage rack.

From the shadow of the train's half-curtained window I sat watching them as they moved off along the platform, chatting brightly to each other, and threading their light summer raincoats through their arms. They were looking ahead for someone they were obviously expecting to meet them; then, on seeing them, they hurried along more quickly.

At last, when the carriage was finally empty, I went to collect my trophy; stuffed it into my pocket; stepped confidently out of the carriage, then made my way with steady strides towards the station's exit.

My friend, Thelma Rillington, came to visit me the other day. I've asked her if she would mind ringing me first, but she mostly ignores that. She just came bouncing in with a thousand shopping bags in her hands and over her shoulders; then plonked herself down on my bed, which also serves as a sofa.

'My God!' she said, as she made herself comfortable, pushing a cushion out of the way. 'How on earth you can live like *this*, Eddie, I don't know. You've got so many *things*!'

'I like things,' I answered defensively.

'Oh, darling, I know you do. *Everyone* knows you do.'

'And at least it's tidy.'

'Well, yes – it is,' said Thelma with a slight scowl, as she glanced about the room, 'I *suppose*.'

'What do you mean, "I *suppose*"?' I replied aggressively.

'Now, sweetheart, don't get touchy. It's not good for the heart, you know. Shall we have a drink – a coffee?'

'If you want a coffee, go and make it yourself,' I said, hoping to make her conscious of the annoyance I felt, but knowing it was something she wasn't good at.

'Oh, it's going to be one of *those* days, is it?' Thelma replied, as she pushed herself up out of the sofa and headed towards the kitchen.

'Look, Thelma,' I called out, 'I didn't *ask* you to call round – did I? And you didn't ring or anything. So why should you assume that I'm glad to have you here?'

'Oh, ducky, don't be like *that*,' she said, appearing in the kitchen doorway with the coffee pot in one hand. 'You know you like seeing me.'

'But that's not the point,' I answered, still sore at her and at her habit of taking over the place. 'The point is that I *might* have had someone with me – mightn't I?'

'Such as?'

'Such as Mark, for instance.'

'Oh, *him*.'

'What do you mean by that "oh, *him*"?'

'Well, you aren't seeing *him*, are you? You aren't going to have *him* round here?'

'Of *course* I am. I like him. It's inevitable that I shall have him here eventually. And how can you speak like that, Thelma, in such a derisory way, about someone you've never met?'

'Now, Eddie – don't start using those fancy words of yours to me. Just the Queen's plain English, please, so we can all understand . . . If he *had* been here, this Mark, and if the two of you *had* been up to something, you wouldn't have answered the door – would you? – and I'd have just left. And you know darned well that I would have.'

'I'm not so sure,' I threw at her.

'Oh, *Eddie*!' she exclaimed with a deep, throaty laugh, looking at me, all aglow with a kind of powerful, motherly light that lit up her skin and that caused the rather beautiful set of beads she was wearing to acquire new depths of purple and gold.

'Now, darling,' she said, as she brought the coffee tray into the room and placed it on a table close to the sofa, 'you must tell me all about him. You *do* have sugar – don't you, pet? You shouldn't, you know, and *I* shouldn't either. It puts the pounds on. But indulgences are good for you at times. So what's he like?'

'Mind your own business,' I said. 'I don't ask you about *your* love-life, so please don't ask me about mine.'

'Oh, I think you *do*, Eddie. Or perhaps you don't need to, darling, since I'm always spouting on about myself so much.'

'Perhaps,' I said, still not feeling comfortable with her.

'Well, what about him, then – this Mark? What's he like? What does he do?'

'He works.'

'Well – that's *something*, isn't it? You been to bed with him yet?'

'Look, Thelma, I'm not getting into that kind of talk. You know too much. And you can't keep things to yourself. One word to you about something personal and the whole of London gets to know of it.'

Thelma didn't answer this. Instead, she stretched towards the coffee pot and began pouring out the coffee. Then she suddenly stopped and looked directly across at me, and said, in a totally different voice, 'Are you all right, pet?'

'All right?' I answered. 'How do you mean?'

'Well, you're so touchy today. Is something wrong? Are you in trouble, perhaps? Is something bugging you?'

Thelma has this uncanny sense of timing, and can use it, as she did then, to undermine any defences I might form. For the truth was that I had been thieving that afternoon, and for once had almost been caught – *and*, moreover, by a store detective. And with this being such an unusual thing to have happened, I was feeling deeply unsettled.

'I'm just not myself, Thelma,' was all I offered as explanation. 'I don't know why. It's not to do with Mark, though – he's nice, really decent. It's just that – well, sometimes I feel shaky, insecure. It's just me, I guess.'

Thelma allowed her gaze to linger on me a while longer before she accepted what I had said. 'Well, as long as it's nothing serious, pet – that's the main thing. But you will speak to me about it if you want to – won't you?'

'Thanks, Thelma,' I answered. 'If I want to, yes, I will.' Then I began to sip my mug of coffee and she began to sip hers, turning towards her shopping bags as she did so;

and in a while, as part of a ritual we observed, I knew she would be showing me the various purchases she had made, and asking for my approval.

The night I left home – I am now going back in time again – is often in my mind; so often, in fact, that I sometimes wonder if there are others who have experienced such a thing: the almost compulsive recollection of one particular memory. It is as if I have to relive it and to go *on* reliving it, perhaps for all my life.

The pattern is always the same, down to the smallest detail. I see myself hoisting my suitcase out of my wardrobe with great care, in order to avoid making a noise; then putting on the coat I had decided to wear and slowly buttoning it up; then creeping my way stealthily down to the first-floor landing of the house – where, because its door had been left ajar, and because its curtains had not been drawn, I could see the moonlit spaces of the sitting room, with its chairs and sofas all placed in their different positions, and their small wine tables set beside them. Then, through the windows of the room, I could see the ghostly image of the town's small square, with the eerie town hall clock – lit, as it always was at night, by a pale-green, yellowish light – telling me that it was now gone half-past one; and seeming to assure me that everyone must now be fast asleep, and that the only encounter I was likely to have would be with the odd stray dog or cat. There were no sounds, except for the faint snoring that came from my father's bedroom and the steady, familiar tick of the big grandfather clock that stood below me in the hallway.

I can see it all so clearly, so vividly; and not only see it but re-experience it as well. All the emotions that are attached to it are ever active in me, it seems; creating shudders in me, even now, as I see myself descending

23

the second run of stairs that led directly into the hall; then opening the main door of the house that gave on to the square, before stepping across its threshold into the street.

I find it hard to believe that I was then just sixteen years of age – and moreover (for my parents travelled very little) had never been much more than fifty miles from home; either to Exeter or to Taunton, or at the most perhaps to Plymouth. London and what its reality might be was something quite intangible. It was just a name, a kind of legend, that had now become a goal. Yet I can recall how confident I felt that I would get to it eventually, having estimated that I could easily walk the two miles or so to where the main road led to Taunton. From there, I felt sure I could hitch a lift from someone; that perhaps some car-driver or some lorry-driver would help me on my way. It was only the time factor that worried me: whether I could get to Taunton quickly enough. For once there, in a town of that size, I would find places in which to hide; and even get work perhaps of a kind; and with it some cash that I could then add to what I had with me in my suitcase.

I can still see my father's eyes as he sat facing me over breakfast. Grey-green in colour, with a curious overlay of gold, they seemed at times almost reptilian, and they gave no notion of what his thoughts might be, or his feelings. He never smiled – or never at me; and certainly not at my mother. He did laugh occasionally, in a rather dark, almost abstract manner, but only when with men, never in the company of women. Not even when with Amy, who had clever means of humouring him when he was in one of his difficult moods, and who was able to relieve the tensions there always were in the house when the spankings first began. Eventually, as I grew older, the spankings became such serious beatings that at such moments my mother would always closet herself in her room, and Amy would quake with anger in the kitchen, knowing she dare not interfere, since my father always made it clear to her, as he also did to me, that the punishment he was meting out was just: that stealing was a crime, that it was a law being broken. 'Do not take things that do not belong to you,' he would repeat over and over again, as he removed the broad leather belt he wore around his waist. 'Do not *steal* them,' he would say, as he raised his arm to strike. And full of anger though she might be (and I am sure my mother was as well), Amy believed that, severe though the beatings were, and perhaps a form of cruelty as well, my stealing was more than shameful and that what my father did was necessary.

I said I would need to be generous towards my father and not depict him as an ogre; but I cannot do that yet: I can only see how difficult it is going to be. For even now, I cannot bring myself to imagine what his reactions must have been the morning after I left home, when he, or Amy, or my mother, discovered the note I had left for him in my bedroom, saying that I was sure of what I was doing: that I didn't hate them – meaning my parents – or anything like that; but that I just felt that I didn't fit, had been a disappointment to them both and needed to get away. I was quite capable of looking after myself, I said, and would write to them in a week or so to assure them I was all right – which, in fact, I never did; although I did send a note to my aunt, saying that none of them was to worry.

I would be in touch, I had written, once I had a permanent address, which, in fact, by chance I soon had. For on the road that night I had been given a lift by someone – a stocky, middle-aged van-driver; who had said to me, after he had listened to my story and to my reasons for leaving home, that although he thought what I really ought to do was turn back, if I felt sure of what I was doing he would help.

'In what way?' I had asked.

'Well,' he said, once I was seated beside him in his van, 'you'll need somewhere to stay – won't you? – once you get to London; so here's my address . . . You can stay with me – south of the river, in Battersea . . . Near the Dogs' Home,' he added with a quick laugh; which was, as I soon learned, a more than appropriate place for him to live. For I had noticed that his van smelled strongly of dogs – that it reeked of them, in fact – and I couldn't help asking him what he did.

'Walk dogs,' he answered, with another quick laugh. 'I always have done . . . I'm not going there now, though,' he went on (meaning to London), 'but if you'd like a lift from Taunton with me tomorrow, I'll give you one.'

'To London!' I exclaimed.

'Yes. That's where you're heading for, isn't it?'

I told him that it was.

'Then be at the bus station at eleven,' he said. 'I've got to go to my sister's now. She lives near here. But I can't take you with me, not at this time of night. She's such a bossy thing, she'd be packing you off home in no time. But if you're at the bus station tomorrow at eleven, I'll pick you up from there.'

I couldn't believe my luck. Just a few hours of waiting was all it was going to mean (for it was already after three) – and I felt that I could easily find some way of passing the time until then; and of getting some sleep perhaps as well; although I can recall thinking it rather odd that the man should be going to visit his sister at such an unusual hour.

'I was due there at ten,' he said, as if reading my thoughts, 'but my van gave up on me, the other side of Barnstaple.

And it took time to get it fixed . . . She knows, though,' he said. 'I've rung her; and she told me she'd wait up – which she probably has done, as we've not seen each other since Christmas.'

It wasn't long before the road signs showed that we were about to arrive in Taunton.

'Now, son, you will be all right, won't you?' the van-driver asked me anxiously, as he dropped me on the outskirts of the town. 'Look, there's a barn over there,' he said, pointing towards a farm that lay just a few yards from the road, and beyond which there was a large, iron-roofed shipping.

'It's a shipping,' I said, in a rather knowledgeable fashion, having heard the soft lowing noises of cattle.

'Whatever it is, you'll be safe enough in there . . . Just go quietly. And make sure no one sees you when you leave. You look respectable enough, but at *your* age you'd soon get reported to the police . . . If someone asks you who you are or what you are doing, tell them the truth: that you've got to be at the bus station at eleven to meet *me* . . . Say I'm a friend,' he added, 'because that's what I am, you know. Just think of me like that.'

The man's name was Rufus. He had told me this soon after I had climbed into his van; and I knew instinctively that I liked him. His calling me 'son' had also had its effect; for I felt that, unlike my father, who was so impersonal and aloof, he was caring and warm-hearted, and because of that I could trust him. Also, I could see in him, I believed, the free, uncluttered spirit I was hoping to become; for he gave the air of having few ties, few emotional commitments of any kind, and that perhaps animals more than humans were his true friends.

'Good luck, then,' he said, once I had climbed out of the van carrying my suitcase in one hand. 'See you tomorrow, at the bus station, at eleven . . . Ask anyone,' he added, 'they'll tell you where it is. And there's only *one*,' he called out as he drove off, nodding at me with a cheeky kind of smile – as if he knew somehow that I was destined to play a part in his life; and which, for a short while, I was.

That night – or that morning, rather – I slept the sleep of the dead. A great wave carried me in my dreams to the shelter of a small cove, set between heavy, amber rocks; and there I rested, and slept, and woke and slept again, so that my outer and my inner lives were one. When I finally awoke the sun was already up, and I could hear early morning movements in the farm. First, those of a tractor passing quite close to me before it moved off into the fields; then the barking of some dog and of someone telling it to stop; then the noise of what I believed to be a bus, passing close to the farm along the road where Rufus had dropped me during the night – which too soon faded away, returning things to silence.

It was a beautiful day. Peeping through a chink in the shipping door I could see that a soft blue haze of mist lay in the valley beyond the farm, through which, from the chimney of a small cottage, smoke rose steadily into the sky.

Don't forget what Rufus said, I recall telling myself. If someone questions you, tell them the truth – that you are on your way to meet a friend who is taking you to London. And armed with that idea, and after I had combed my hair and had brushed myself down and had made myself look respectable, I slipped quickly away, seeing no one and hearing nothing. Then, walking as if I was some student, perhaps, who was setting off for school – or, more probably, for college (since I was tallish for my age) – and feeling proud of myself as well for having done what I had just done in leaving home, I made my way into the town. Freedom, I thought, was something wonderful, and no one could rob me of it now. I was just one night free of my past — of its shade, its shadow and the awful loneliness of my youth — and ahead of me lay only hope, and perhaps too, I dared to think, some kind of happiness.

III

IF I HAVE found it difficult to write about my father, it will be no easier, I expect, for me to say things about my mother. For what is there that one can say about someone who lived such a guarded life; who seemed to have so removed herself from the present? Yet she casts no great shadow in my mind. Unlike the memory I have of my father, the one I have of my mother bears no great weight, calls no real attention to itself. My main picture of her is of someone tall, slim and rather elegant – for she dressed herself with care; and usually in darkish colours, or sometimes just in black, with the relief of a small pattern, perhaps, that offset the amber beads she wore most days, or the rather splendid set in lapis lazuli that she wore only occasionally, and that had been given to her by a friend. Her shoes, too, were smart – well cut; stored neatly on wooden shoe-racks in the large wardrobe that lined one wall of her bedroom. Not that she was sober or over serious in character, for she laughed quite a lot at times; and when she did, it was a light, silvery tinkle of noise that breathed its way into the air and then was quickly gone.

Sometimes, when I was doing my homework in the dining room (as opposed to in my bedroom) and my mother happened to be with Amy in the kitchen (discussing household matters, perhaps, or having a chat with her about local things) I would hear this tinkling laugh of hers: hear it rise, break, fall and then be gone. And I would often wonder what the cause of it had been: what Amy might have said to bring it on.

When I was small – in my infant years, I mean – I must have spent a lot of time alone with my mother, because she had been much less reclusive then, and I know that she took me out for walks most days, usually to a small park that lay on the north side of the town, where she would sit and watch me play. But the odd thing is that I cannot remember it with any clarity. Nor can I remember my mother clearly at all when at table in the dining room, having lunch or supper (for she was never there at breakfast) with my father and myself. The only moment when I can picture her with precision is when she came into my room to say goodnight. Then she suddenly comes into focus, as she pushes open my bedroom door and crosses towards my bed. Then I can see how soft, how very gentle, were her eyes; how truly kind she was, how thoughtful. She did care for me – I am certain of that, for she used to ask me questions about school; what I had done that day; and sometimes she would even tease me a little as well; and those moments are very precious to me. They didn't last long, however, for she would soon withdraw, having patted me lightly upon the forehead, and occasionally having pinched my cheek and smiled.

Why was she like that, I wonder? I cannot put down the extremity of her reserve entirely to my father; for it's not as if he bullied her or anything like that. It's not as if they quarrelled – had fights or words. It was just that she seemed to have accepted, and to have done so without question, the strictness of the order he had imposed upon the house: the regular mealtimes; the ten-thirty bedtime for them both – and, until I had reached my teens, the much earlier one for me. The order too of the occasional supper parties that they gave when they would entertain their friends – if one could quite call them friends – and when I could see how proud he always was of her; of her looks; of the general dignity of her carriage; and of the quiet, steady way she had of conversing and of discussing things. In a sense, they created an atmosphere between them of marital harmony and calm; and no one could tell, I am sure, how maimed they both had been by someone or by something when they were young, and how in retreat they really were both from themselves and from each other.

No, it is the memory of my father that so clings to me – and will not let go of me, even now. His image is still there – fixed, set; grey, grim; almost gruesome at times: a picture that I cannot look into and explore; cannot see beyond the surfaces that ever twist and turn towards me; forcing me to confront its eyes, its nose, its mouth, its slightly protruding ears; and be forever watching them, waiting; hoping for some smile, some sign of joy.

Having put pen to paper in this way and having at last begun to release what there is locked away inside me – boxed up and parcelled away in my mind – I realise how much there is that I need to set down. I suddenly think of Charlie, for instance. I've said nothing as yet about him; yet he's been a part of my life – or he was for a short while. I have spoken of Rufus, at least, but as yet not said what a good friend he proved to be when I went to stay with him in Battersea, in his roomy garden flat that was just a few streets south of the Dogs' Home, where it seemed that all the strays of London were gathered, waiting for their owners to collect them. And in a way, Rufus's flat was a miniature version of that place; for not only did he walk dogs each day for a living – ten or twelve of them at a time – he also owned quite a number of dogs himself. Some of them were strays; some he had owned since they were puppies – and they seemed more attached to him than the rest. And it was into this canine world that he brought me after the long drive from Taunton the morning I left home.

I can remember it so well: arriving in London in the half-light, then driving south across the river into Battersea; where Rufus turned into a short driveway and parked his van at the side of the building in which he lived, close to an enormous, dark-green holly bush that was already showing some berries. At the first sound of his motor his dogs began to bark and yelp from inside the house, and to paw at the french windows facing the garden — which were then opened by someone who allowed the dogs to come racing out, jumping up against Rufus as he locked the doors of his van.

'Everything all right?' Rufus asked, as a big, burly man of about fifty appeared. 'Been any trouble?'

'None,' the man answered. 'Just that old fart across the way — that's all. She's been round complaining about the dogs again. I told her to piss off, and she did.'

This was Charlie — Charlie Garrett — and I noticed that, as he peered at me from beneath the brim of the thick tweed cap he was wearing, his eyes seemed quickly to sum me up.

'Who's this, then?' he asked Rufus, with a sharp nod towards myself.

'His name's Eddie,' Rufus replied. 'That's right, isn't it, son? And I've brought him back with me from Taunton . . . Left home, he has, on account of his father; so I've told him he can stay here.'

Charlie gave a grunt, then looked at me a second time. 'What's wrong with 'ees father?' he asked.

'Bit of a bastard, it seems,' said Rufus. 'I've told him he can stay here until he's sure of what to do . . . I'll get him work, if I can — with Len, perhaps . . . You *can* wash dishes, can't you, son? . . . You ever washed 'em? In a restaurant, I mean?'

I don't know how I responded to this; probably by saying that I hadn't done so before, but that I was ready to try anything. For in less than a week, I think it must have been, I was doing just that – washing dishes in a small restaurant run by a man called Leonard Rillington – who, I was to learn later, was Thelma Rillington's husband, and was to become one of my greatest friends.

''Ee looks green to *me*,' Charlie then said to Rufus, again peering at me from beneath the brim of his cap. 'Been bashed about a bit, too, by the looks of him,' he added. 'Your old man beat you, did he? Your dad, I mean. Did he? Did he beat you?'

I hesitated before replying to this, and I recall wondering why it was that Charlie had so many keys attached to his belt; and also why a large, silver whistle hung on an ochre-coloured cord against his chest. And why it was too that the untidy hairs of his beard seemed to be bothering me.

'I think he *did*,' Rufus said, guessing that I couldn't cope with Charlie's question. 'Isn't that so, son?'

I nodded to this, feeling, as I did so, that I had in some way betrayed my father.

'Mine beat *me*,' Charlie then said, in a rather sober tone of voice, 'but you'll get over it in time, lad – don't worry. He can't get at you now. Not here. That's the main thing. Rufus'll see to that.'

I remember just smiling at this in reply, as Rufus played with his troupe of dogs, who were still excited by his arrival. Charlie stood watching him and then turned to me and said, 'Takes some lookin' after – that lot.' (By which I presumed he meant the dogs.) 'Aye, it does,' he said, as I smiled nervously, uncertain of how I was meant to relate to him. 'Aye,' he said. 'It takes a lot.'

And when Charlie said that and tugged at the peak of his cap, and rubbed one hand over his beard and his moustache, while Rufus bounced about the garden with his dogs, I sensed that I was safe: that I had found somewhere where I could settle for a while. I had no great liking for dogs, but as they raced around the garden in a ring and leapt into the air and barked, I felt that they and Rufus – and Charlie too (if he lived with Rufus, that is, which I can recall thinking that he might do) – would all act as my protectors. Not once did I imagine that they might mean danger of any kind – or harm – odd though the relationship between the two of them seemed to be. Charlie did make me nervous, as I have said, but I sensed that this was only due to the strangeness of his personality, which was something totally new to me; and which, as yet, I was finding it difficult to understand.

'Shall I take the lad in?' Charlie then called out to Rufus. 'Get him some tea?'

'We'll all have tea,' Rufus replied, as he began to settle his dogs, rubbing their ears and patting their heads. 'Won't we, fellas? Eh? . . . We'll all go in, eh? We'll *all* have tea.' With which, Rufus picked up my suitcase, which had been left standing beside his van, and we followed Charlie into the house.

'Newspaper's down,' said Charlie, with a quick nod towards the floor as he stepped across the threshold of the garden window. 'Scrubbed the place out this morning,' he said to Rufus.

'It's to take the mud from the garden,' he said to me, indicating a path of folded newspapers that crossed the room's linoleumed floor.

What next? Well, I seem to be quite good at describing things, so I'll try to describe Rufus's flat. It was roomy, as I have said – by which I really mean that the few rooms there were were large – and on the ground floor of an old Victorian house. There were two bedrooms, one of which was given to me; and Charlie and Rufus (as I discovered later that first night) slept in separate beds in the other. There was a huge kitchen, a kind of dining room next to it, and then an enormous room at the back – the one that looked out upon the garden. The place was sparsely furnished, mostly with second-hand, scrubbed-wood tables and chairs; and just a few dumpy armchairs covered in a heavy, tufted fabric that had abstract patterns woven into it – probably bought in the 1930s, I should think, or perhaps during the war. The flat was clean – kept so by Charlie, I realised, who used to go from room to room each day with a mop and a pail of steaming water into which he had plunged a bar of carbolic soap. The shiny, linoleumed floors were also patterned – mostly in browns and oranges and the occasional line of blue – and there was always a slight smell of disinfectant in the air. This, I believe, was intended to offset the smell of Rufus's dogs, which, in spite of the regularity of Charlie's moppings, tended to predominate. It wasn't an unpleasant smell, however. In fact, in the mornings, when I got up and made my way to the lavatory (there was no bathroom, by the way, and we all washed at the kitchen sink) I used to think what a pleasant atmosphere this mixture of smells created: one of cleanliness and care. Even the sheets on the beds smelled slightly of carbolic, for on Mondays Charlie would always strip the beds, boil up great saucepans full of water and fill the huge porcelain sink in the kitchen, where he would wash the sheets with his soap. Then wring them with his hands before hanging them out to dry.

I can see him so well: how he would carry the wet sheets with him in a large wicker basket; then stretch to peg them out carefully on clothes-lines in the garden. Then, once he had done that, how he would collect a few wooden clothes-props that were kept at the side of the house, and use them to push the sheets higher into the air.

He was in no way self-conscious about what he was doing. Sometimes, he would sing a wartime song; occasionally, one from an earlier period, such as 'Goodbye Dolly Gray' (he taught me the words of that), or 'I'm in Love with Two Sweethearts', which was a rather sloppy song about a man's love for the two women in his life – his mother and his wife. Rufus never – or certainly hardly ever – helped Charlie with these chores, but eventually I helped a little, and I enjoyed it; and I could see – or I could guess, at least – that Charlie was pleased to have my company.

'Can you bring out a few more clothes-pegs, Eddie?' he would sometimes call out to me from the garden; or he would ask me to help him move a bed, or a cupboard, perhaps, so that he could more easily mop beneath them.

Each morning, immediately after breakfast and a long time before I had to go off to work in the restaurant, Rufus would leave in his van, his dogs barking and yelping after him from behind the ironwork gates at the side of the house. And he hardly ever came back until close to teatime, when I, of course, wasn't there. For I had to leave for work at about four in the afternoon; which meant that I saw very little of him – just for the hour or so at breakfast-time, and during most of the day on Sundays, which was looked upon by all three of us as being a day of rest. Then, the dome-shaped Bakelite radio would be switched on and the flat would be alive with the sound of music – mostly light-classical pieces; or things such as Victor Sylvester's dance band, which I enjoyed.

'You dance?' Rufus once asked me; which I had to answer by saying no, since I had never been taught to dance, or allowed to go to the local dances at home. 'You should,' Rufus replied. 'It's good for you. Shakes your bones up – don't it, Charlie?' To which Charlie answered with a laugh and a jerky nod of the head.

I often thought that the two of them were wanting to get up and dance together in front of me and that I was perhaps inhibiting them.

'Does Charlie dance?' I asked Rufus one day, thinking that my saying this might make things easier.

'Oh, yes, Charlie dances – don't you, Charlie?' Rufus said, with a wicked twinkle in his eye. 'You should see him dance the tango . . . Here,' he said, suddenly grabbing hold of me and pulling me to my feet, 'I'll show you.'

The sharp rhythms of a tango could be heard on the radio, and he then tried to teach me the steps of the dance – how to bend and occasionally swoop – laughing excitedly all the time, as Charlie tapped his feet.

But that only happened once; and for most of the time that the three of us were together, Rufus and I would read and Charlie would clean and cook; and sometimes (I never knew what prompted it) would suddenly race out into the garden to blow a sharp blast upon his whistle; to which, almost in chorus, the dogs seemed to reply, with a series of noisy snaps and barks.

'Bloody hell,' Charlie might say, as he returned; or 'Pumping fuckin' thunder'; or 'The bloody bastards' – for what reason, I didn't understand; but it did show me that his mind was in some way unbalanced and that he was preoccupied by something: something that rose at times to the surface, and which, for a while, the sound of his whistle appeared to release.

It does seem strange, as I write of it now, to think that I lived with these two men, and that I so quickly fitted in with them and their habits. I was then still very young, as I have said, and many things that I know now I had no knowledge of at that time. It never occurred to me, for instance, that Charlie and Rufus might have been lovers. I did know – vaguely – that men lived together, and, I presumed, had a sexual relationship of some kind; but as yet my experience was far too limited for me to be able to embrace such an idea, and because of that, I probably blotted it from my mind. What I do know is that I was happy: that despite the general emptiness of the flat, despite the scrubbed-wood furniture and the patterned linoleum floors, I felt that I was somewhere where I belonged – and both Rufus and Charlie helped me to believe that too. Without any words being said about our relationship, or about the change it must have meant for them to have me living there in the flat, they allowed me to fit in, and for all three of us to feel comfortable there together.

Perhaps, in a way, I came to think of them as parents, and they in turn to think of me as their child. Whatever, we were a happy family of sorts; and when I eventually moved here, to where I am now (just north of the river in Chelsea), I felt sad.

'Come and see us some time,' Charlie had mumbled, as I had climbed into Rufus's van.

'Oh, he won't do that,' Rufus had answered, catching hold of one of my ears and giving it a quick, affectionate tug.

And that, alas, is what happened; for fond of them though I was, and attached to them though I had become, when I set off in Rufus's van, with his dogs barking noisily behind us, I knew as I turned to see Charlie staring at us, with no smile at all on his face, nor wave of the hand to say goodbye, that I would not be able to return: that that part of my life was over; that it had served as a means for me of my breaking free of the past, and that it was now something I could not re-enter.

That sounds selfish of me, no doubt, and perhaps unkind. But I know that neither Charlie nor Rufus really expected to see me again. Just once since then, when I was taking an afternoon stroll in Hyde Park, have I seen Rufus. He was in the distance, walking his dogs. Not his own dogs, but the ones that he collected from different houses and took for walks each day. And I wanted to call out to him and ask him how he was, and how Charlie was as well. But something forced me to hold back, and I strolled on, noticing as I did so that a man who was sitting close to me on a park bench had a packet of cigarettes lying beside him with a silver lighter perched on top of it. And then (as, with me, it so often can) my mind began to toy with the idea of how I might make the lighter mine.

Sometimes, when I am walking along, of an afternoon, perhaps, when the sun has gone around to the west and there are deep shadows lining the Embankment, I think to myself that if I *had* to make a choice, then of all the places in the world in which I could live, this would be the one I would prefer – here in Chelsea, just a stone's throw from the river. I've been here so long – for almost twenty years, it must be – and I feel that this is where I belong. Not that the flat itself is very attractive. It has no outlook; no garden – just a small, enclosed patio that never gets the sun; a largish living room that also serves as a bedroom; quite a decent-sized kitchen, beyond which there is a bathroom and a toilet; and then just one smallish lumber room, as I call it, at the back, in which I store a lot of my 'things' – to use Thelma's name for them – mainly packed in boxes that stretch from floor to ceiling. None of what I think of as my 'collection' bears any trace of the original owner, by the way, for I have been meticulous about that; so that if, by chance, someday, someone gets to know of my compulsion, there will be no means of their discovering to whom the objects belonged.

It is a strange form of illness, it seems to me, in that I can hardly call myself a kleptomaniac. For instance, I have never felt a need to steal from people's houses – when I am visiting them, that is. I don't go around picking up people's ashtrays, or pieces of jewellery that are left lying around in living rooms and such. It has to be in a public place; on a bus, for instance, or a train; or in a shop or a store – or even on a park bench. Why I suffer from this I do not know. Analysts would tell me, I am sure, that it has to do with insecurity of some kind, and with the fact that my father's beatings had been so sadistic that they had robbed me of my confidence and had fuelled my obsession. But I don't know that I agree too much with that sort of idea. Certainly, it has nothing to do with monetary gain, for I have never sold any of the things that I have stolen. And even when there have been notes – banknotes, that is – in a wallet, I've usually left them where they were; so that they too, in time, become part of the beauty of my collection.

Occasionally, when I am alone (and this tends to be late at night, when my mind is inclined to wander), I enter, by way of my fantasy, this treasure-house of mementoes: not by actually looking at them, or by handling them physically (I rarely do that), but by recalling them mentally, which I am able to do, and remembering, because I always can, the different excitements that became attached to them through the acts of making them mine.

I regret to say that I seldom think of the people I have robbed, or of the pain it must have caused. I appear to have built some kind of defensive screen in my mind against doing that; which obviously makes me not a nice person – or not a very moral one, at least. However, that is me – who I am and how I am made. Nor will I attempt to excuse myself by saying that the things I stole were always small – such as books, purses, wallets, etc. (just once, quite a valuable watch) – all of which, I have to say, had been left lying unattended. None the less, I do sometimes wish that I had kept the names and the addresses of some of the objects' owners. For just occasionally, in an odd flight of the imagination, I see myself returning some of my trophies through the post, with no letter of explanation attached to them; so that I can then picture in my mind the looks of puzzlement this would engender – having things that had been lost and perhaps forgotten, arriving through the letter box.

However, that is enough of that; there are more pressing things I need to write about: such as my parents' deaths, which occurred just over a year ago, each within a few weeks of the other.

Their deaths upset me a lot and caused me a great deal of inner turbulence – and they still do; so it's not going to be easy for me to describe the experience in words. But it has now suddenly occurred to me that their having left this world could possibly be a reason for my having begun to release these thoughts. Certainly, had they still been alive, had they still been here, I know that I would never have spoken – written (not even secretly, as I am doing now) – about my private life. Not just about my thieving, I mean, but about other things as well: my experience with Tom in the woods, for example; or about how, when she came to see me the other day, I spoke to Thelma about Mark, saying he might have been here – with me; and about which she was rather dismissive, I thought.

Well, I'm very pleased to be able to say that he is coming here for supper tonight. We met only a month ago, in a bar near Piccadilly. It's not a very attractive place, but I go there from time to time because it is used by men who like men – in the way that I like men myself; and we had a chat and seemed to like each other. So we arranged to meet again – in the same bar – a week later.

Then (this was just a few days ago) we went to a film together – not a very good one – and had a bite to eat afterwards. And then – well, I asked Mark if he'd like

43

to come here, and he said that he would. For supper, I said, rather rashly, for I'm not a good cook; with the result that I spent much of the day yesterday wondering what I might give him. Spaghetti bolognese, I thought – but then decided against it, because it means doing things at the last moment. So I've settled on a soup (a tinned one with a dash of wine in it) and then cold meats and things like that, and an Arctic Roll for a pudding.

I'm hoping it will be all right, because I like Mark a lot. He is as tall as I am, which is a relief; a year or two older, which rather appeals to me; works in Fulham (in a wine bar, I gather) and lives there too, so he's not very far away. *And*, to my surprise, he finds me quite good-looking, which I am not. I'm not bad-looking – not ugly; but good-looking is not what I am, which at times adds to my lack of confidence, I suppose. Anyway, he's coming, and it'll be the first chance we've had to be intimate together, of which I can honestly say there is every sign of our wanting to be, but one can never tell.

Right now, though, when there's a little time to spare before Mark arrives, I'm going to write about something else – something I've not spoken about as yet – which is how very bright I was at school when I was small: at primary school, that is, where I was always top of the class and when the reports that I used to bring home each term to my parents said that I excelled in almost everything.

Looking back at it now, it seems impossible to believe that this was so: but it was: and I am sure that both my parents must have been proud of me. Not that either of them actually said that they were; but I used to learn, either through Amy or through my aunt, that they were pleased; and I'm sure that it gave them reason to think that I had some kind of academic future ahead of me – which perhaps at the time was true. Where, in this regard, I felt that I became a disappointment to them both was later, when, after having won a scholarship that took me on to a good grammar school, where I knew that they expected me to do well, things began to change. Not immediately, but within a year or so of my being there. For by then I was no longer getting good reports from my teachers, and 'unable to concentrate' or 'very poor' began to be the type of comment made about my performance. And soon, from being considered bright and very intelligent, I was thought of – and, indeed, came to think of myself – as being something of a dunce.

I can now see that this sudden change in my status as a scholar was caused by two quite different things. One was that, as I approached puberty, I became confused about my sexuality and had no one with whom to discuss it; and the other was that, by then, the compulsive desire to steal had become something much more serious and more disturbing than the occasional childish prank that I had always made it out to be when I was small. Instead, it had became something that seemed to take hold of me and possess me. Also, of course, the punishment that I received each time from my father (each time I was caught, that is) had gradually become more violent and had taken on an element of shade – of shadow – far beyond what might be considered normal. For I knew perfectly well that what I was doing was wrong; and I knew as well that it would often lead to quite painful physical punishment. But that seemed almost to egg me on; as though I desired unconsciously to provoke my father into humiliating me, which is – was – I suppose, a form of masochism.

And, to a certain extent, both these things still play a part in my life today. I am still not at peace with myself as far as my sexuality is concerned; still feel guilty that I am not what is called normal; still feel – even now, when they are dead – that I don't want my parents to know what my sexual tastes and preferences are, which makes a decent relationship virtually impossible. And although I do genuinely hope each day that things will change and improve, and that I will somehow master my obsessions, there are no signs as yet that I shall, and it appears to be something that I am stuck with and might have to endure for all my life.

Having said that, however, I have noted of late – really recently, I mean; almost since meeting Mark, now that I come to think of it – that certainly as far as my thieving is concerned, the compulsion has slackened its grip on me a little. For there have been times during the past couple of weeks when I have managed to control it for a while, and have been able to withdraw whatever projection I have formed upon what, for a brief moment, has become the object of my desire. And that is a noticeable change. Yet I am far from mastering it. I am sure of that. The habit has now become so ingrained in me that it is much like the habit of smoking, which people find so difficult to give up; and it makes me see myself as someone in a real mess. However, I do form friendships – at least, of a kind – such as the one that I have formed with Len and Thelma; so I can feel proud of myself about that. Proud in their case because they are both such lovely people, and because, no matter what, the three of us know that we will always be there to support each other, should the need for it arise.

I've just read through some of the things that I have written down so far, and realise that they give an impression of me as being someone rather sad. Well, I suppose I am, in a way – or I am underneath, at least: but I don't think that I give the effect of being so on the surface. And certainly I have never heard anyone say of me that I am a sad person. In fact, I think that while most people see me as being a little sober, perhaps, in character, they also see me as quite a cheerful person on the whole; and quite a humorous one as well; so it would seem that the act of writing things down brings out the sides of us that are hidden – or it can do. Oddly – because I didn't *plan* to set down these thoughts, but just fell into doing so, as it were – I now realise that at the very back of my mind – buried in the subconscious, I suppose one could say – I've always had ideas about becoming a writer. My failures at school, however, which were a part of my reason for leaving home (and why I had said in the letter I left for my parents that I had been a disappointment to them both) led me away from the possibility of ever fulfilling that desire. Yet I do like books and words, and I read a lot. One of my favourite authors at the moment is a writer called Ivy Compton-Burnett (the stress is on the first syllable of the last name, by the way; or so I am told by a friend of mine who admires her work). She's not very popular, and she has even said of her books that if someone should happen to pick one of them up they will find it difficult not to put it down. A strange figure she is, but a respected one, and she has an unusual style of writing that appeals to me. She's now very old, but I used to see her at times in the street, when I'd been visiting Len and Thelma in Kensington, just to the west of Gloucester Road, which is where she lives; and I've heard her talk on the radio, in an interview, in which she was being questioned about her work, and I found her fascinating. Her books are full of quips and quotable sayings, such as 'Happiness is not the only thing in life . . . and laxness and liberty may not always be conducive to it' – which, it would seem, as far as happiness is concerned, is something I might think about.

IV

IT MUST HAVE been three weeks after I had left home and moved in with Rufus and Charlie that I again wrote to my aunt giving her my address, and repeating what I had said in my previous letter – that, dramatic though it had been, I was sure that what I had done had been right – and assuring her that not only did I have a comfortable room of my own in Battersea, but that I had regular work as well. I didn't say what type of work it was, because I didn't think that my aunt would approve very much of my washing dishes in a restaurant; nor did I mention Rufus and Charlie. I did say that if she wanted to write to me from time to time I would always answer her – and that if my mother wished to write too (I said nothing about my father) I would answer her as well. And this arrangement has continued until this day, and I am grateful to my aunt for it. My mother did write once, saying how upset she and my father had been made by my decision to leave home, but she didn't plead with me to come back and I had the impression that she was in some way relieved by what had happened, in that it had reduced the tension there was in the house, and that this had made her life more comfortable.

'You know we will always be pleased to see you,' she had written, but it somehow didn't ring true; and through my aunt I learned that after the initial upset of the event, and the temporary scandal caused in the local community by my suddenly leaving home, my parents' life soon settled into a quiet, non-eventful one.

'We go there sometimes at Christmas,' my aunt wrote, 'and we have quite a pleasant time. But if I mention you, or say you have written, I get very few words in reply.'

Did I miss my parents? Yes – I did, at times: my mother in particular; and at night, during my early days in London, as I was settling down to sleep, I would often picture her pushing open my bedroom door and crossing towards my bed, then bending over me to pat me lightly upon the forehead before saying goodnight. Who I missed more was Amy; and at the end of my letters to my aunt, I always sent her my love. (And I've always sent Amy a card at Christmas, to which she always replies; usually with a brief note giving me her news, and sometimes adding that Tom, her elder son, sends wishes.) But neither Amy nor my aunt ever spoke of my father in their messages. That seemed to be a subject best avoided; and it was one, I have to admit, that I never raised. For the division between us was so great that it seemed a topic best forgotten; and the only time that I ever saw my father again was on his deathbed, when, having lost his voice and unable to communicate through words, he looked at me with a fierce, impersonal stare; as if to say that my having entered this world as his offspring was beyond his power of comprehension. I think that I did attempt to smile at him – and, for a brief moment, I felt a desire to take hold of one of his hands; but I succeeded in doing neither, and recall how he suddenly turned away from me to stare across the room; then drew his legs up towards his chest to lie curled beneath the sheets, as the room began to darken, with me waiting patiently for the night nurse to arrive and for my bedside vigil to end.

That was a year ago, and my father's death had been preceded by that of my mother, who, having gone to bed one night with no sign of being unwell, had simply slipped away.

'She just faded out,' my aunt wrote in a note she posted me that same day. 'But you will come – won't you, Edwin?' she had added (meaning to my mother's funeral). 'Your father's illness weakened her, and he can no longer speak. So do come – come and make peace with us,' she said, 'before it's too late.'

And it was this plea from my aunt that finally broke my resolve, and helped me to take the difficult decision to return to the house in which I grew up, and in which, in fact, I had been born; now, no longer young and into my thirties, and looking, alas, rather too much like my father for comfort.

'Oh, my goodness!' my aunt declared, as I stepped off the train at Taunton, where she and my uncle had come to meet me. 'You look exactly like your father.' Then she broke into tears and threw her arms around my neck and kissed me; and I did my best to adapt to the shock of seeing them both again, and of how savagely time had affected them. Then to the further shock of only recognising with some effort that the stout, elderly lady standing behind them was Amy, dressed in a thick, tweed coat and a knitted Fair Isle beret.

I can still see her large, watery eyes, searching desperately in the person she saw confronting her for the boy I had been when I left home.

'Tom's here,' she said nervously, nodding towards the station car park; and she accepted the formal kiss I gave her, then wiped her eyes with a handkerchief. 'Your aunt and uncle don't drive any longer,' she added.

'Too old,' my uncle said, with a quick laugh.

'Not senile, though,' my aunt then added.

'No, no,' my uncle replied, 'far from it!'

All three of them burst into laughter and the blood rose quickly to colour their paper-thin cheeks, as, from behind the hazy mist of a dull November sky, the sun attempted to smile at us.

'Oh, my God!' exclaimed Amy with a shrug, her younger self breaking through the barriers time had imposed upon it, 'it's bloody *cold*!' Affecting a shiver, she trotted along more quickly until, beyond us, close to the car park's entrance, I could see a burly man in his mid thirties, perhaps, who was standing close to the bonnet of a large station-wagon, and staring at me in a rather puzzled way.

'Eddie?' he asked, as he stepped towards us, and a dark lock of hair that suddenly tumbled over his forehead helped me to realise who it was.

'It's Tom,' he said as he shook my hand, as if confirming his identity. 'We'll put the oldies in the back, shall we?' he added with a warm smile and a nod of his head. And then, to my surprise, once he had settled the three of them into the roomy seats at the back, and once he himself had climbed into the driver's seat, where I was seated beside him, he placed a hand lightly upon my thigh to give it a quick, affectionate squeeze. Then he laughed, asked if the passengers at the back were all comfortable, before, with a sudden roar of the car's engine, he drove off.

How painfully difficult it is for me to write about this, for I did feel shamed by my long absence from home. Had my parents really been so negative? I kept asking myself. Hadn't I been too severe – too harsh – on them both? and on Amy too? These thoughts came flooding into my mind as Tom drove us away from the car park to head for the heart of the countryside; until suddenly, as we turned a sharp corner topping a hill, we were given a view in the near distance of a great valley – where, nestling among the moorland hills that surrounded it, I recognised the town in which I had been born, and the familiar sturdiness of a church tower that soared free of its smoking chimney-stacks. And all the emotions of my childhood years returned to me, filling my mind with memories of things past.

But was it really that to me – home? I asked myself. It had been so long since I had been there that I found myself half dreading the thought of seeing my parents' house again, and of encountering in it its all too familiar rooms; and I knew too, of course, that my father lay there ill and unable to speak, and that soon I would have to find a means of relating to him.

'Well, you've come back at last,' my aunt stated quietly, breaking the silence that had fallen between all five of us in the car.

'About time, too,' Amy added reproachfully.

'Oh,' said Tom. 'He's had his own life to get on with, haven't you, Eddie?'

Again he put out a hand to pat me upon the thigh. At which point I noticed a golden band on one of his fingers, which might have been a wedding ring, and sensed, at the same time, that he had some kind of intuitive understanding of exactly what I had become. It was a type of knowledge that he appeared to share with his mother; one that was independent of words – of language, of any kind of verbal exchange; and I couldn't help wondering why it was that he sometimes sent wishes to me at Christmas. Was it because I entered his thoughts from time to time, as someone who held a meaning for him? A sentimental one, no doubt, but a meaning, none the less; and one that I felt glad of.

Thelma has called to see me again, which makes it the second time this week. She just 'popped in', she said, 'for a cuppa' – which wasn't a very apt description of what she did. Blew in, or bounced in, would be more accurate

53

– and, using all the spill of her matronly charm, took over the place in no time.

'You all right, pet?' she had asked, as she was busy dumping her things and making herself at home.

'Don't I look it?' I answered, wondering what she was thinking.

'Oh, yes. You do. You look fine. Different, though. Definitely. Something's happened – hasn't it?'

'Such as?' I asked.

'Well, how would I know, sweetheart? But *something* has, by the looks of it.'

'I'll make some tea,' I said, 'or coffee.'

'Oh, will you? . . . Well, that will be nice. Coffee for me, though, at this time of day.'

'Coffee then,' I said, as I slipped away into the kitchen.

'Mark been here?' Thelma called out.

'What?' I asked, pretending I hadn't heard.

'That Mark,' she said. 'Has he been here yet?'

'Yes,' I answered, not wanting to lie.

'Oh – *has* he!' she said. 'Well, how did it go? You two in love or something?'

'Thelma!' I answered, pushing my head around the open kitchen door; 'Mind your own business, please,' not wanting to betray the fact that Mark and I had spent the previous night together and had realised that we liked each other a lot.

'But it *is* my business,' Thelma persisted. 'I'm your best friend, remember? Except for Len, of course. You like him more than you like me, because he doesn't ask awkward questions.'

'Oh, Thelma!' I called out to her with a laugh. 'Trust *you* to say a thing like that.'

'Well then, tell me. Seriously, Eddie, have you met someone you like at last?'

'Maybe,' I said, as I brought the coffee in from the kitchen.

'Well, that's lovely,' she said, her eyes all aglow at the thought of romance.

'Is it?' I said.

'Well, of course it is. It's lovely to have someone who means something to you: something more than just sex and bed.'

'Well, darling – *you* should know about things like that,' I answered her teasingly, knowing she doesn't quite like it if I begin to answer her back.

'Should I?' she said, a little curtly.

'Yes,' I said, 'you should. And I mean it nicely, by the way,' which made her smile.

And as we sat there having a gossip and talking abut the various things we had done that day, I saw how much I appreciated the genuine warmth of her concern. 'Don't tell Len, though,' I said, as the subject again came around to Mark. '*Please*, Thelma – not yet.'

'If that's what you *want*, of course I won't,' she answered. 'It'll be just between the two of us.'

'For the moment,' I said, since, as yet, my feelings about Mark weren't really definite; and because I wasn't yet feeling at all confident as to what his were about me.

'Well, whatever – it's nice,' said Thelma, bringing the subject to a close. 'It's good. Things are changing, Eddie – for the better. I can see. There's colour in your cheeks for once – do you know that? . . . Lovely coffee,' she said, as she sipped from her mug and then dunked a chocolate digestive into it. 'Nice,' she said. 'Really lovely.'

'I'm glad,' I answered – as the question suddenly entered my head as to exactly why it might be that in the various notes she had enclosed with her Christmas cards over the years, Amy had not mentioned to me once that her eldest son had married.

★   ★   ★

That first night of my return is fixed permanently in my mind: the memory of it ineradicable. It had been arranged that Amy would help me to settle in and would cook me some supper; and that Tom would return later with my aunt, who would then stay to keep me company until the night nurse had arrived. Which meant that once Amy had gone off to busy herself in the kitchen, I was alone in the house – or I had the *sense* of being alone, since although I knew that my father was there as well, his illness confined him to his room and I knew that there was no danger of his appearing and confronting me.

It was a strange experience being able to move from room to room without my parents being around. I recall how I went upstairs to the sitting room and, on opening its door, found that it had hardly changed at all. The furniture appeared to be in exactly the same positions; and the big, glass-fronted cupboard, which more or less lined one of its walls, contained the same things – the same volumes of Dickens and Trollope that my mother used to read, the same sets of silver tea-services and their accompanying trays, the same set of dark green cabbage-leaf china, arranged in rows on the upper shelves. And it seemed to match in almost every detail the night-time image of the room that I had carried in my mind, and had kept and guarded and had returned to so very often.

Now it was late in the afternoon, not one o'clock in the morning; but with it being mid November it was already dark, and the square looked exactly as I remembered it from all those years ago, with the town hall clock still lit by a pale-green light. Only now there were people about and the shops were lit; as were the windows of the Castle Inn, where my father so often went for a drink – particularly on market days, when its bars were open all day.

★　　★　　★

'Excuse me,' I heard a voice say behind me, startling me.

I turned to see a neatly uniformed nurse who stood facing me in the doorway.

'You must be Mr Carpenter's son,' she said.

'Yes, I am,' I replied, not having taken in the fact that my father was so gravely ill that a nurse was required throughout the day as well as the night; yet, had I but thought of it, he could hardly have been left alone when my aunt and uncle, and Amy too, had all been there at the station to meet me.

'Your father's asleep,' the nurse said, 'and I'm about to go . . . But if you would care to sit with him –'

'Oh, well,' I answered, 'if he's asleep . . .'

'Yes, I understand,' she said. 'My name is Beth. Beth Williamson.' She thrust out a hand towards me. 'Nurse Williamson, if you like,' she added with a smile.

'Thank you, nurse,' I said, feeling a need to be a little formal with her. 'I shall be here for a few days. Perhaps a week. But you know that, I expect.'

'Yes, I do. Your aunt told me . . . It will give her a rest. She's been so good, you know – quite wonderful – what with your mother dying as well.'

'I am sure,' I answered, not wanting to be made to feel too guilty on account of my long absence from home. 'She was always close to my mother.'

'And to your father too, it seems,' the nurse replied.

'Well, yes,' I said, thinking it wasn't true: for how could I imagine her, or anyone, having a close relationship with my father? 'My father as well,' I said.

That was then, however, as I have said before, and now is now, with both my parents dead and buried; the house sold; the furniture disposed of, except for things that my aunt and uncle wanted, and a few small pieces that I now have with me here and one or two other things that are left in store. And that is all there is to remind me of my childhood days in the country. It had been a shock to me, having both my parents die as suddenly as they did, and neither of them of a great age. It seemed that my life was full of savage, sharp divisions, of untimely partings and farewells. I told my aunt that it would mean a lot to me if I could come down and visit her from time to time; and since she seemed more than pleased by this idea I am planning to go there next week. That will be in the heart of the countryside – not in the town – and I am looking forward to it. For when I was small – from the age of about ten, it must have been – I was allowed to visit her – and my uncle too, of course – on a Saturday, walking the two miles or so through the narrow country lanes to their farm, which lies on the east side of the moor. There, different memories will be awakened, for those Saturdays are almost the only times in my childhood when I felt free and really happy. It was a happiness I felt I had to conceal, however, out of a fear that I might be robbed of it; but I knew that once Saturday's breakfast things had been cleared away, and after my mother had called me up to her room, in order to give me some message, perhaps, or some small present for my aunt, I would set off; even in winter, when there might be signs of heavy snow. It now seems strange to think that I should have been allowed that weekly excursion; but there – I was; and I recall that I was never afraid (not that one had much cause to be in those days) of being a young boy on my own. Most of the boys who went to my school felt a similar sense of confidence, and we all moved freely about the countryside. I might pass a farmer on the way – on his tractor, perhaps; or, just occasionally, tramps, or 'travellers', as they were sometimes called – odd-looking men who toured the area's farms and villages looking for work, never staying anywhere long, and whose lives seemed to be ones of being forever on the move. But they were never rude or threatening. They might not say a cheerful 'Good morning, young man', as the farmers and their workers did, and would only look at me in order to weigh me up – perhaps to judge by my clothes whether I came from a decent family – but they never made me nervous. If anything, I felt more secure during those walks than I did at any other time in those days. I was alone. There were only the trees and fields and the animals keeping me company. And I knew them all: the black, furrowed earth in wintertime, and the dark holly trees in the hedgerows, alight with scarlet berries; the black crows, soaring on outstretched wings across the frosted moor; the warm brown thatch of the few small cottages I would pass; the barking of dogs, the clucking of hens. Then, when I finally arrived at the farm, the sudden excitement of it all: of the men at work – busy feeding the cattle with a root vegetable called mangel, perhaps; or with flatpole – a coarse cabbage that wasn't thought quite fit for human consumption, yet would sometimes be boiled, then chopped and fried with potatoes to make a delicious bubble and squeak. Also, the bread being baked in a wall-oven in the kitchen – and at Christmas-time, when my uncle and aunt would give a party (to which I was never invited, alas, because it was a party 'only for grown-ups'), the rich, unforgettable experience of the huge, thatched barn, in which the cider-press was housed, being emptied out and cleaned; and its rough, clome walls being whitewashed – or distempered, as it was then called – before being covered with shiny, metallic netting known as chicken wire, through which enormous sprays of fir and shiny holly would be threaded, transforming the barn's spacious interior into a mysterious temple of green.

There was no tinsel, as I recall; no paper decorations of any kind; not even a Christmas tree. Just metal hurricane lanterns that lit the space in a particularly magical way. And then there were the long trestle tables – set out against one of the dark green walls – covered with stiff, white damask cloths, upon which, eventually, when the evening came, great cuts of ham, tongue, pork – a rib or two of beef, perhaps – would be placed; and on which bowls of beetroot and pickled walnuts, and later of junket and sherry trifle, would all be arranged with care, and with a natural sense of the aesthetic.

I so often wished that I could have stayed for one of those parties. But it was not to be. My uncle, who was particularly kind to me, and who was very sensitive about such things, would often say to me, as he was driving me home, 'Pity you can't stay, Eddie; but you'll be allowed to when you're older, you know.'

Now, alas, it is too late. Those days of such country richnesses seem to be over. My uncle and aunt are now too old for it, and are past such things in any case; and I doubt very much that the farmers of that area give quite *that* kind of party any longer – when, according to Amy (who was always employed to help for the evening in the kitchens), drinking and dancing went on into the early hours; and when the bedrooms would be full of card players sitting at small, baize-topped tables that had been set out around the beds. And often for quite serious sums of money, of which I knew that my mother disapproved – since she always told people the next day that she had chosen to 'sit out'.

So – even though there will be none of all this to enjoy, I am looking forward to going there, and to be making a return to somewhere – the only place in my childhood – of which my memories are deeply pleasurable.

I seldom see Len alone. These days, it is almost always with Thelma, when I go to have lunch with them on a Sunday, perhaps; or occasionally to have supper. I stopped working for Len a long time ago, after I was offered a clerical job in an office by someone who ate regularly at his restaurant in Battersea. It's the job I still have – and I took it because it gives me more reasonable hours: the evenings off, for instance, when I can go to the theatre or the cinema, both of which I enjoy. But I miss the talks that I used to have with Len at the restaurant, because he's quite an intellectual and has lots of interesting ideas. He's almost the opposite of Thelma, who is all instinct and feeling; which is why they make such a good couple, I suppose. He does come here at times, but, unlike Thelma, never without having arranged to do so beforehand. I like him so much, and often think to myself how lucky I am to have such a friend. I've learned so many things from him. He's helped me to look at paintings and to think and to read books; although, to show how different we are in our tastes, he can't understand at *all* what I see in the work of Ivy Compton-Burnett. 'Can't be bothered with it', is the way he passes it off. And Hitchcock too – the film director – he can't understand why it is that I like him, or why I like his films, rather. 'Just thrillers – murder pictures', he says, and can't see that they have a strange depth – and, as I see it, are the products of a very deep form of possession.

Perhaps it's the darkness in me that allows me to appreciate them: the fact that I know only too well how very powerful any form of compulsion can be. How it forces one to project one's feelings on to things that are outside of one's self, and so robs one of one's centre. However, there are many other areas of taste in which we agree – more than enough – so I can't really think that those differences are ever likely to spoil things for us. The one whom I am more concerned about is Thelma; about how she would cope with my having a relationship – one that becomes a permanent one, I mean. It's ungenerous of me to imagine it, I suppose, but I somehow think that although she'll profess to being pleased, and will say that it is all she ever wished for, she won't be so underneath; and in time might even become a source of trouble. As yet, though, she and Mark haven't met. Len has met him – but only once, and just by chance; because Mark was about to go home from here one Sunday when Len arrived. But that went well. They talked, soon laughed, shared a few light jokes about me, and that was that. There were no hints of anything else – of any displeasure. Len never says, for instance, as Thelma will often say, 'Oh, that Mark'; as if he was not to be taken seriously, and was someone soon to be got rid of. On the contrary, I saw in Len's eyes – in his smile as Mark left – that he was truly pleased for me; and that he really did hope, as much as I have begun to hope myself, that Mark and I will continue with our relationship and that it might eventually become a stable one; and that, with time, we might become just as much of a couple as are Thelma and himself.

V

HOW BEAUTIFUL CHELSEA is, or at least this part of it close to the river. On my way home each day I fall more and more in love with it as I leave the main shopping street and turn into one of its side streets, and as I see, perhaps, as I did yesterday, the early evening sunlight gilding the brick façades of its houses. How can it be, I ask, that I should find myself here in the heart of London, when I was born and grew up in the country? There are no fields, none of the open spaces of the moors. Everything is contained, confined, boxed in.

Quite close to me, just a short walk away, are the grounds of the Royal Hospital, where a breeze blows in from the Thames, and where, in early summer, the famous Flower Show is held; and it's a pleasant place to go to – particularly on a Sunday, when the city is quiet, and when there are often children playing, accompanied by their parents or their nannies. It's helped me to appreciate urban life; made me see the city as a garden that has to be cared for and looked after, as opposed to something wild. Heather, which is such a part of my childhood memories, would seem out of place here, in this environment. Flowers and plants seldom spill randomly, as do the wild ones of the countryside; they sit formally in boxes, or in beds in the parks and gardens. And in a way, I prefer this. Prefer it, because it reflects the way my life has gone; the way I have made my choice – my direction. For I have come to love the life of the city: the weekend rides on the buses, whizzing me to Trafalgar Square and the National Gallery, which I now visit quite often. For I have become fascinated with painters and their paintings, and often wish that I had been blessed with some kind of artistic talent myself. I even think at times that I should go to night classes, perhaps, and try my hand at it.

Mark paints. Not very well, I'm afraid, but he likes painting a lot; so there we have something in common. I'd been with him to the National Gallery the other day and I foolishly spoke about it to Thelma. 'Oh, very artistic, are we?' she had answered with a smirk, and really offended me, in the way that she so easily can. I don't know why it is that she reacts to things in that way, unless it is out of fear; because, in this case, she has so little sense of visual things. Or it could be jealousy, I suppose. 'He's been to the National Gallery,' she said to Len, when I went to have lunch with them last Sunday. 'With his friend, Mark,' she said. 'Didn't know he had leanings in *that* direction – did we?' So I've said no more to her about it; particularly because Len didn't speak up and support me, as he so often does. But that could be because he too isn't interested much in things to do with the eye; books and words being his world. I did say to her – to Thelma – 'I bet you've never heard of Piero della Francesca,' trying to put as much bite into my expression as she puts at times into hers; but it didn't work. 'Is it likely?' was all she threw back at me, as she disappeared into the kitchen.

No, I thought to myself, it isn't. She's so blind about so much, which makes it all the more difficult to introduce her to anything new. She's so conservative, so very set in her ways.

However, the main thing is that Mark knows who

Piero is all right. He's one of his favourite painters, in fact, as he is mine. There's a marvellous picture by Piero in the National of Jesus being baptised, with a near naked man at his left standing close to a winding stream; and he – the man – is wonderfully painted: as, for that matter, are the three angels standing at Christ's right: three extraordinary columns of pleated drapery, and with such serene, impersonal expressions upon their pale, pink faces.

Then, in the middle of the picture, there is Christ himself, with St John standing close to him and about to perform the ceremony. It's difficult to describe, but there is such a very pure, such a very refined, air about everything. It seems to me that it is quite unlike the work of any other artist of that time – or, indeed, of any time. Painters like that don't appear very often it seems; don't reach that point of clarity, of a wondrous kind of abstraction, and of achieving such a high form of spiritual order.

Another painter I like very much is Stubbs (which shows that my taste is rather classical, I suppose). There's one of a lady in a carriage that is being drawn by two incredibly well-painted horses. Jet-black in colour, and so dreamlike, so poetic. I have found that if I study this picture for a while, it surrenders a strange, uncanny meaning: a sense of timelessness; of it being not about the things of this world at all, but about some other place and time that is both constant and eternal, and that exists beyond the world of the appearance that the conscious mind sees and knows.

It's one of my favourite paintings. And Titian's *Portrait of a Lady* is another. That is something quite different, in that, in a way, it is so incredibly present – there in the room, hung on the gallery wall. But it too achieves that sense of timelessness; the image being so brought down to essentials that it generates a power of its own; so that I find myself thinking about its literary subject matter hardly at all. I have no fantasies about the lady who, in her plum-coloured dress, stares so uncompromisingly out of the picture-frame. It simply doesn't concern me who she might have been or what her station in life had been. Somehow, the structure of the image overcomes all that, and I find my eye wandering appreciatively and in admiration from one part of the picture to another; from the extraordinary sensitivity of the lips, to the fine gold chain around her neck, to the sudden, dramatic slash of white that is provided by the lining of her sleeve and that explodes out of the dark plums and greys of the painting's overall colour. And all this has been part of my learning – of my growing up; and a result of the decision I took to leave home and to make a life for myself in London.

Oh dear, though: now that I've got into the habit of writing things down, there seems such a lot that I need to say. I was even thinking at work this afternoon that if I decided to set down here in detail *all* the memories that have piled up in me during my thirty-odd years of existence, this journal of mine – this notebook – would become something much bigger than the Bible!

Every day of your life things happen: things that are interesting; and that mark, if you take a good look at them, the continual change taking place in your development. I've just remembered a chap called Patrick Flanagan, for example, who, for almost a year after I moved here from Battersea, lived in the flat above me. I *have* to say something about him, for he certainly played a part in my growing up, and in my getting used to life in the city. An Irishman, as is pretty obvious from his name, he lived alone, after having parted from his 'lady-friend', as he spoke of her – who (or so he said) left him because of his drinking. And I can recall as if it was yesterday the moment when he came knocking at my door.

'I'm your neighbour,' he said, 'and I'm there in the flat upstairs. You'll not be minding, I hope, my coming to call on you like this . . . My name is Patrick,' he added, with a winning smile. 'And my guess is that you'll be new here in the city . . . You like eggs?' he suddenly asked.

'Eggs?' I answered, unable to imagine why he should be asking me that question.

'Yes, eggs,' he said. 'I've got four dozen of 'em, and don't know what to do with 'em. Won them, I did, as part of a prize – in a competition. Asked me what I'd do with eggs, they did, and I said "Smash 'em". So they gave me money – a cheque, if you can be thinking of such a thing – and these eggs. A bloody great boxful of 'em.'

He laughed nervously as he said this, causing his tall, wiry frame to shake and his rather protruding ears to flap. 'Because I answered this advert, you see, asking you what you do with eggs, and I said "Smash 'em", just for a bloody joke – so there's going to be this big poster or somethin' with eggs runnin' down it, and tellin' you that eggs is good for you, or you should be going to work on one, or something like that . . . So,' he went on, having paused to catch his breath, 'I was thinkin' that maybe you'd care to help me get rid of some – scrambled, perhaps, or in an omelette – so we could get to know each other a little.'

This quick gush of words had rather startled me. First of all, because I could hardly believe that what he had been telling me was true; and also because I could smell that he had been drinking, and wondered, with my being so young at the time, and so inexperienced as well, whether I ought to accept his offer or not.

He didn't look dangerous, however: he wasn't untidy-looking or dishevelled in any way, or needing a shave. In fact, he looked bright and perky and in an odd way rather attractive. So I said to him 'When?' – meaning, when did he want me to join him for this feast.

'Well, now, I thought,' he replied with a disarming grin. 'It'll be gone midday, and you'll have eaten nothing since breakfast, I'll be thinking. So what about now – eh?'

'I'd – I'd have to change first,' I said, just to gain time.

'*Change*?' he said, looking me up and down. 'What for, for fuck's sake? You're tidy as a pin-box. Come as you *are*, son.'

'Edwin,' I said, realising that I hadn't yet told him my name.

'Oh, so it's Edwin, is it?' he answered. 'Well, Edwin, you'll do fine for me as you are. But if you *want* to put on something else, just come up to me when you're ready.'

I thanked him and off he went; and I recall thinking as he left that London life for me seemed to be full of eccentric characters. Already there had been Rufus and Charlie. They weren't exactly what one would call everyday types; and now there was this Irishman – Patrick – who had come knocking at my door and had gabbled on to me about eggs. Still, it was interesting, and certainly unlike anything I had experienced in the country, or was ever likely to experience, I thought, had I stayed on there – unless I had got to know some of its tramps, perhaps, or gypsies. So I changed and went, feeling a little nervous, as I recall, but driven on by curiosity. For the very idea of my having a neighbour of that kind seemed an excitement in itself. It was all part of my new adventure. I was still working in Len's restaurant in Battersea, and had to leave for there at about four in the afternoon; but with my not having found enough courage as yet to go out and explore the city (other than the streets of my immediate area, with which I had quickly become familiar) my days at home seemed long; and the only people I saw socially at that time were Len and Thelma. I saw Len each day at work, of course, but only spent time with both of them on a Sunday, which meant that the other days of the week were often quite lonely ones for me.

As I locked the door of my flat and turned to mount the stairs to the upper floor, I began to picture in my mind what Patrick's flat might be like. Would it be dark, light; tidy, untidy? Would there be paintings, books? Would his crockery be clean? (This was a thought that quite worried me.) Would his clothes be strewn about his room, or rooms? Did he use gas for cooking, or electricity?

It is amazing how quickly the mind is able to explore an unknown space in this fashion, building pictures of it and furnishing it in one's fantasy. But it seems to me that the fantasy and the reality seldom match. One's idea about how a thing will be, or how it will look, tends to be an illusion that will be shattered. Certainly mine was regarding my neighbour's rooms and habits of living. For nothing there was as I had pictured it in my mind. There was none of the darkness I had settled upon; no pictures, very few books; and he cooked by electricity, not gas. Nor were his clothes strewn about the place, as I had half made up my mind that they would be. And, moreover, instead of it being dirty and unwashed, his glassware and crockery were spotless.

'Like to keep the place shipshape,' he said as he let me in, seeing me looking about in astonishment. 'Clean, trim,' he said. 'There's nothing like order, you know . . . Now, Edwin,' he asked, 'do you think you'll be having a tot of whisky, perhaps?'

I said no to that, for I drank very little. 'Just water, please,' I added, 'if you don't mind.'

'Oh, I don't mind, lad – Eddie, I mean. I don't mind at all. I'm not lookin' for you to be a drinking buddy, you know. Just someone to talk to from time to time, and to stop me from feeling lonely; which I do feel on occasions . . . You kept?' he suddenly asked.

'Kept?' I answered, having no idea of what he meant.

'Yes, kept? Or a rent-boy, or something?'

'Rent-boy?'

'Jesus,' he said. 'Don't you know what a rent-boy is? Well, it's someone who sells himself – rents himself out to other men: that's what it is. You never heard of a rent-boy, laddie?'

'Eddie,' I said, hoping he would soon get used to my name.

'Eddie,' he repeated.

'What for?' I asked. 'What do they sell themselves for?'

'Oh, Jesus!' he exclaimed, ruffling his blue-black hair. 'Look – forget it. You don't know, and it's as well that you don't. How old are you, for fuck's sake?'

'Sixteen.'

'What!'

'Sixteen,' I repeated.

'Well, you don't look it. You look about eighteen, I'd say, or even older. Holy Moses! And you say you're new to London – to the city?'

'Yes,' I replied.

'From where?' he asked.

'From Somerset. From the West Country . . . What do they sell themselves for?' I asked a second time, wanting to have him tell me, in spite of the fact that I had half guessed by then what the term meant.

'For sex,' he said. 'That's what for. For sex. For men to have sex with them – for money.'

'Oh,' I answered, the idea of such an arrangement intriguing me. 'Where?'

'Where what? Where do they do it? Where do they sell themselves? Or where do they have sex?'

'Sell themselves,' I answered.

'Look, lad.'

'Eddie,' I said.

'Look, Eddie, you'll know all about this in time. If you're new here, you'll soon learn about things like that. Not because you'll be doing it yourself – or I *hope* you won't – but because every city person gets to know of it. You queer, perhaps?' he asked, looking directly at me. 'Is that what it is?'

I didn't answer this, much as I understood what the word meant. I just paused – then looked up at him and asked if he was himself, which caught him out.

'Jesus!' he said, as his face coloured. 'You're a bit of a card, you know . . . Look. How do you like your eggs? And what about a drink? Don't you drink at *all*?'

'Just water, please,' I replied. 'You asked me that before.'

'Oh, look,' he said with a laugh, 'I'm not wantin' to lure you into bad habits. But what about a beer, Eddie? I can't think that a beer would do you harm.'

'A beer?' I said. 'Well, yes – perhaps,' since I felt it was somewhat rude of me not to be joining him.

'Well, a beer, then,' he said, 'and I'll have a whisky.'

'Thanks,' I said.

'Oh, no thanks, son – please.'

'Eddie,' I said.

'Eddie,' he answered. 'No thanks – please. I can see that we're going to get along fine together. I'll take you out; show you the city: get you about a bit. What've you seen of it so far?'

'Not much,' I answered. 'In fact, I haven't gone far from here as yet. I like Chelsea, and I work at night in a restaurant south of the river – in Battersea; and only have Sundays free, when I see Len and Thelma, my friends . . . Len owns the restaurant where I work, where I wash dishes.'

'Oh,' Patrick answered, handing me a drink, 'so that's what you do, is it? That's why you're home during the day . . . Well, take a sip of this. Good stuff, it is. The best bottled beer you can find . . . Here's to us, then, Eddie.' He raised his glass and stretched out to pat me upon the shoulder. 'Jesus, Eddie,' he said, 'you're quite a card, you are. You are, you know. I can see . . . Oh, Jesus! – what a lot you have to learn, and what a lot it is too that I'll be havin' to teach you.'

Patrick made the most delicious scrambled eggs, which we had on toast, and I enjoyed his company a lot. I knew that I needed him and felt that he had a genuine need of me. In his case, it was just for company, I thought, for I could tell that he was lonely. But what I needed was someone who would act for me as a guide and help me to know the city.

Was he unemployed? I recall asking myself, as he had said nothing to me about work that day. And if he was, then how could he afford whisky? But the following morning I heard him leave his flat quite early, and I rushed up the stairs to speak to him.

'Patrick,' I said, a little out of breath, surprised to find that he was wearing workman's overalls. 'Thanks for yesterday. It was smashing,' I said, making a joke that I thought he might appreciate.

He chuckled at this. 'It was nothing, Eddie,' he answered. 'You must come again. We must get to know each other better . . . Have to go,' he said cheerfully. 'Work, you know. I'll see you later.'

I watched him as he jogged off down the street, his hands thrust into his pockets, and thought how much I liked him: that there was something special about him. At which point he turned to look back at me and to smile and wave a hand.

'Later, Eddie,' he called out. 'I'll see you later.'

I lingered until I saw him hop on to a bus, then turned to go inside and down to my flat, where I soon made myself some breakfast.

VI

A BIG SHOCK for me during the past year – an enormous
one, now that I come to think of it – was my discovering
that my father died almost penniless. Even the house wasn't
entirely his, but was partly owned, I learned, by my aunt
Sarah – my mother's sister.

This was something I hadn't allowed for. I had long
accepted the idea that my father might not mention me in
his will, however much I was sure that my mother would
have wanted it; so I wasn't expecting to inherit anything
from him at all. But the knowledge that he had debts, some
of which were quite large, suddenly changed my view of
him. For rather than the stern, moral figure of authority he
had always stood for in my mind, I now saw him as not having
been a crook exactly, but certainly something of a gambler.

'My goodness, yes,' my aunt had said to me, once we
had been told the contents of the will, which had made
my aunt and I the sole inheritors. 'Didn't you know? He
was always like that; always living beyond his means . . .
Your dear mother – it worried her such a lot. He did have
money at one time, of course, that he had inherited from
his family. But he squandered it. And he never did much
in the way of business. You do realise that, I suppose. He
used to call that room at the back of the house his office,
but it was hardly ever used as such. It was more of a betting
shop, if anything, for he was always backing the horses. Just

occasionally, though, he'd do well at *something*: *some* bit of business. Some deal he'd fixed over a sale of cattle, perhaps, or land. But he relied mainly on the pension he had from the war. The one for the injury to his leg. It wasn't much, though, and after their first few years together, I don't think that he and your mother had an easy time of it; which is why they never went anywhere much – never travelled.'

As my aunt was telling me this, I began to feel a kind of sadness regarding my father – something I'd not felt before in my life. For suddenly he was flawed. Suddenly he was an impaired, an imperfect, being, in the way that I was one myself; and I saw us as being more alike than I could have imagined.

'The house will just about pay off all the debts, though,' my aunt assured me, 'so we don't need to worry about that. And there'll be its contents as well. We can share those – do what we like with them. Even sell some of them, if you want us to: if you are in need of money, Eddie.'

I explained to her that I had to live carefully, since I did only clerical work and my salary was small, but that I had savings, none the less (this didn't include my 'spoils'), and wasn't in desperate need of money.

'But you could do with *some*,' my aunt had added, 'I'm sure. So that's what we'll do – shall we? Everything's more yours by rights than it is mine, in any case; so just take what you want, Eddie dear. What do *I* need it for, at *my* age? Just leave me a few pieces, perhaps, as a reminder of them both, and keep the rest for yourself.' Which is exactly what we have done; and this coming weekend, when I've arranged to go down to the country to visit her, my aunt and I are going to decide what to do with the few things that are left. Then it will be finished. My father's estate will be cleared – settled, over and done with; and in just a little more than a year after his death.

★   ★   ★

'You didn't like your father, Eddie – did you?' my aunt had said to me after the funeral.

'No. I didn't. He frightened me,' I answered truthfully.

'Frightened you!' she exclaimed. 'Why? Because of the spankings when you were small – the beatings?'

'Yes, partly,' I said, 'but also because I never heard him say a good word about me to anyone.'

'Oh, Eddie, he must have,' my aunt replied. 'I'm *sure* he did. He wasn't *that* bad, was he? Surely he wasn't.'

I can't remember what I said to this, but she then asked if it had really been because of my father that I had left home.

'Yes,' I said. 'It was.'

'Oh, dear,' she replied, 'I'm sorry. I wish I'd known, wish I had realised. I could have told you things about him that might have helped.'

'I don't think anything would have helped, Aunt Sarah,' I answered quietly. 'Those beatings were savage. Even now, the thought of him and the look in his eye frightens me, gives me the shivers. He'd force me to push down my pants and then he'd take off the belt he always wore around his waist.'

'Oh, Eddie, dear,' my aunt replied, her eyes suddenly wet with tears. 'How hurt you have been.'

'Yes, Aunt Sarah – I have. Those things stay with you, you know. And even when he was dying it didn't change. I tried to make amends. I did try to touch him to show some affection, but he still rejected me and turned away.'

My aunt said nothing to this. I recall that we were seated at the dining table in my parents' house, upon which we had arranged various papers; and that the light outside was just beginning to fade.

'Oh dear,' my aunt said at last, suddenly rising to her feet and crossing towards the window. 'Why is it that family things so often have to be like this?'

'I don't know, Aunt Sarah,' I said, rising to join her and to look out at the town square, where the shops were now lit, and where, floating against the evening's lavender sky, the town hall clock was soon to become the ghostly, pale-green moon with which I was so familiar. Then, for one brief moment, my aunt took hold of one of my hands and pressed it between her own.

'Bless you, Eddie,' she said, as the tears began to roll steadily down her cheeks. 'Bless you,' she repeated, then released me and turned to leave the room.

.

VII

THE LATEST THING regarding Mark is something that happened only last night, after we'd been to see a film together and had strolled back to my flat, where we'd had supper. For as we came in, he suddenly caught hold of me and asked me if I loved him.

'Well, do you or don't you?' he said rather aggressively, when I gave no instant reply. 'It's one or the other, Edwin; either you do or you don't. I want to know.'

I was absolutely caught out by this. We've been getting along so well. It's all seemed so easy – so very natural: sharing our tastes, our likes and dislikes; discussing this, discussing that – exploring each other's bodies when we're in bed. But now, this suddenly seemed an invasion of all that, and I didn't know how to cope with it.

'Do you need to ask that, Mark?' was what I came out with eventually. 'Do you need me to answer that question?'

'Yes,' he said – again very aggressively, 'I do.'

'Mark – look,' I said, 'you want me to be truthful, don't you? You don't want me to tell lies; to say something I don't feel, just to please you – just to make you feel comfortable.'

''Course I fucking don't,' he said gruffly.

'Then, if that's the case, I can't honestly answer your question. I can't, Mark. I'm sorry, but I just can't.'

Mark looked crestfallen.

'You see, I don't think I really know what love is,' I said, filling the silence that had fallen between us. 'If it's enjoying each other, as we've been doing now for some weeks, then – well, the answer is yes. If it's something else – something more mysterious – then it's not something that I know about . . . Perhaps it's because I had so little love when I was small,' I said. 'I know I'm not very passionate – I'm aware of that. But I can't *make* myself be so, can I? I'm doing my best, Mark.'

It was my saying this that seemed to prevent things from going really wrong, because he suddenly looked up at me and smiled, and stared deeply into my eyes, as if he was needing to find me there at some new level.

'Doing your best, Eddie?' he said. 'I *know* you are,' and he pulled me swiftly towards him and gave me a hug.

'Supper, then?' I said, once the hug had changed to kisses and the emotion between us had subsided a little.

'Yes, supper,' he said, 'and then . . .'

'Then bed?' I replied, teasingly. 'Is that what you're thinking?'

'Of *course* it is,' he answered, cuffing one of my ears. 'What else, for fuck's sake?'

Today's been such an awful day for me – really bad. Everything seemed to go wrong, even the weather, which began bright and cheerful enough, but then turned suddenly dark and savage, with such heavy rain in the afternoon, and so cold for the end of March, which it is about to be tomorrow. Going out like a lion, I suppose. That's what they say – isn't it? And it certainly came in gently enough, with soft, balmy, early spring days, and the parks and gardens bright with cheerful flowers. Well, I suppose it has to happen. I suppose life can't maintain a forward movement for long, much as we might want it to.

The past is always with us, it seems, and there's no escaping it. Yesterday, for instance, there I was full of hope for once, and daring to look forward; and thinking to myself that at least there's nothing really troubling me. I'm going down to the West Country this weekend, and I've that to look forward to. Mark is all smiles again and is wanting to come with me, which I'd like him to do, so that he can meet my uncle and aunt, and see my background too – what there is left of it. I've even told him that I'll take him to the woods where I first learned about sex – meaning with Tom. Mark loved it when I told him about that. 'So romantic,' he said; which, in a way, it was. And I've no money worries either, and might even have a few pounds extra in the bank, once my father's estate has been finally settled – which it almost is, with all the debts having been cleared, and with my aunt having insisted upon my accepting the money raised by all the sales of things in the house that neither of us has wanted: most of the furniture being too large for me and not needed by her; and the silver, too – all of it rather ornate and rather cumbersome. *Also* (and this is what pleases me most) I've managed to speak to Mark about my thieving.

He was shocked at first – really upset; he just couldn't believe that I was a thief. 'You mean, you really *take* things?' he asked. 'Nick things – that don't belong to you?' And I told him how I had always done it. '*How* often?' he asked, almost as if he himself had been a victim of what I had done to others. 'Not *that* often,' I had answered. 'Less now.'

'Less now than *what*?' Mark had almost snapped back at me. 'Less than once a year? Less than once a month, a week, or what?'

'A month, I suppose,' I answered. 'Now, just five or six times a year, I guess.' (Which wasn't entirely true, since, during the past twelve months, it has certainly been more frequent than that.) 'I don't know *why* I do it, Mark. I just don't. My father used to beat me for it when I was small. That's why I left home. Savage it was, the way he used to lay into me.'

'What do you steal?' Mark then asked.

'Oh, anything. It can be anything. A book; a purse – a wallet. Just anything. Once or twice a watch. Nothing really big. Usually in public places, where things are left lying around. And I can't stop it, Mark, much as I try to.'

'But what if you're bloody well *caught*, Eddie?' Mark asked, with a look of such deep puzzlement in his eyes.

'What if I'm caught? Well, I was once – no, twice. Each time by the owners of the things I'd stolen, or was about to steal. But each time I got away with it. Said I hadn't been intending to steal them; simply thought they'd been left lying around and were lost – which in neither case seemed at all a likely story; but they accepted it, together with the apologies I gave – half mumbled; showing, I suppose, that I was something of a case. Not nuts, exactly, but a little strange at the least, which, in this respect, I suppose I am . . . And they looked at me, not in a fearful manner, but more objectively than you'd expect, as if they wanted to distance themselves from me; and by doing this they allowed me to slink away.

'But those are the *only* times I've been caught,' I continued. 'Just once, I was almost nabbed in a store – that wasn't long ago – and – well – the store detective had no proof, because I had managed to slip whatever I had taken back on to its shelf in time.'

'Who else knows about this?' Mark asked, his voice still dark in tone and slightly censorious.

'Who else? Well – no one,' I replied.

'What about Len and Thelma?'

'No,' I answered. 'I almost told Thelma a while ago,

when she saw that I was upset and not myself. But for some reason I suppressed it.'

'But you've told *me*.'

'Yes.'

'Why? Why is that?' I was surprised by the urgency in Mark's voice.

'Because . . . well, because I trust you, Mark – that's why; and because I don't trust anyone else.'

'Not even Len?' he asked. 'Not even Thelma?'

'Not even them,' I replied.

So all that has been good. I've shared my secret at last; robbed it of some of its shade, and it's been a help. But today – oh, today! – a different kind of robbing has taken place; as if some old time-warrior had suddenly stepped up out of the past and given me a right old clobbering. It's been awful. I dreamed last night that I was in an ancient castle close to the sea, its inner walls festooned with mementoes of various kinds: a frayed, decaying handkerchief, one corner of which was knotted (whatever that might mean); one or two hats, some faded and made of straw, with half-dead roses at their brim; some charred-edged letters – things like that. Some babies' shoes, one pair of which was dotted with rhinestones, causing them to gleam and glitter in the narrow rays of light that were bouncing in off the sea through the castle's slatted windows. And this has stayed with me all through the day. The castle's owner following me, menacing me in my mind, no matter what I do.

A girl at work asked if I was well – meaning, in fact, the opposite. 'I'm fine,' I answered, but she looked at me, knowing that I had lied.

'I think you should go home,' she said. 'You're sick or something.' But I stuck it out – went on with my work, which fortunately isn't too difficult, and so struggled on through the day.

What does he want of me? I sometimes ask myself – this tall, bald-headed warrior-figure, whom I have known for so many years. Is he perhaps waiting for some moment when he can triumph – can show me that he has won? God knows. *I* only know that he's a bother in my life; that he's a stalker of my mind – one of its dark night-watchmen. And what I dread most is the thought that one day I might see into his eyes: that one day he'll stare directly at me, and that that will then be that.

Oh dear, though – I so dislike it when I'm like this. But it's such a part of me, I am afraid – this being dragged back into the past and being psychologically maimed by it. I'd like to speak to Mark about it; but while he can just about cope, I think, with the problem of my thieving, I fear that something like this would be too much for him; so I've decided to say nothing. Just that I'm a little unwell, perhaps, and that I get into a bad mood at times – if he notices it, that is, which he might not. Or just say that there are moments when I need to be quiet and on my own.

However, we've not come to that as yet. Today, for instance, we've not arranged to meet – so I'll get past this one; and my writing about it has helped. It's such a wonderful thing, I've discovered, setting things down: committing to paper one's most secret thoughts. It helps you to know yourself better – and what's more wonderful than that? Helps you to cope more easily with that great lump of unknown flesh that we all carry around inside us, it seems. Being so aware of it, as I always have been (partly, I expect, because I spent so much of my time alone when I was a boy), I find I can always recognise it in others. Thelma, for example – she's carrying a great big blubber of the stuff around with her; but the marvellous thing about

Thelma is that, unlike me, she seems not to be burdened or hampered by it at all. She seems able to handle it, carry it with her, sling it around – quickly relieve it with some temper, or a hearty burst of laughter. And Len, too, in quite another way. I know that he knows about this in the way that Thelma does not, because he's interested in things to do with the mind, and knows about the fact that we are all only partially self-aware, and that we all carry about with us this clumsy burden of not-knowing. But *he* copes with it by being patient: by never challenging his self-ignorance and by always accepting it. He won't even let Thelma use it as she would like to do at times, when she wants to upset him for some reason, which she quite often does. Like some hermit-crab, he will back away and withdraw into his shell – and she gives up.

'Coward!' she'll say to him sometimes, when she can't get at him; at which he just laughs, as if to say he'd rather fight another day. Because he'll never let her corner him, I am sure of that.

Anyway, I'm at home now, writing this, and the day is almost done. I've nipped out and bought some fish and chips for supper, and am about to have a bath and go to bed. Once Mark has rung, that is, which he is going to do from the wine-bar where he works. At about ten, he said, and I am quite certain that he will. For that's what I like about Mark; that he always does what he says he will do. In that he's like Len, whereas Thelma will make me promises, such as 'I'll pop in and see you tomorrow, Eddie – after work' (meaning after my work, not hers, for she only does part-time work in the mornings) – which she'll often say to me on a Sunday, and then simply not show up. And she won't apologise for it either. 'We didn't say definitely – did we, sweetheart?' she'll tell me the next time we meet: to which the answer always has to be that we didn't, because she has a way of not defining anything too much; and for which reason I always seem to forgive her.

Mark is good at taking decisions – much better than I am, and at the beginning of last week he had made up his mind that for our weekend in the country he was going to hire a car and drive us there in comfort. And this, I might add, in spite of my having said to him that I liked going to Taunton by train, as I had done for my father's funeral, then going on from there by bus – and also that it was quite a long journey. However, that is what we did – what we have done – leaving London last Friday lunchtime, and returning yesterday, Monday, with both of us having arranged to take the Friday and Monday off from work.

We had a lovely time; something quite special, it was. I didn't think I could be that happy. And I shall always recall the moment when we left Taunton, and saw before us in the far distance the great lines of the Exmoor hills, with the sun sinking behind them, encircled by rings of purple and gold.

Neither of us spoke. The sight before us was so beautiful – so intoxicating. And with his not having been to that part of the country before, I could see how impressed by it Mark was. As we sped along, I turned to look at Mark and smile – just to show how much I was enjoying our journey – when it suddenly struck me, which it had not done before – I can't think why – that there was something about Mark that reminded me of Patrick: the Irishman who used to live in the flat above me.

Was it the whiteness of his skin, which was so heightened by the rich, dark colouring of his hair? Or was it the size of his ears, which were a little over-large? Or was it the general leanness of his physique, which made him look thinner than he actually was?

'What are you looking at?' Mark asked, keeping his eyes on the road ahead.

'You,' I said.

'There are better things to look at than that,' he answered. 'Right now, at least.' Then he chuckled and said no more. And in the way that it can, there suddenly came back to me, from a long way in the past, the memory of a night when I was about to be seventeen. It was the eve of my birthday, as I recall, and Patrick, my neighbour, had taken me out on the town — part of my education, he had called it. We had gone to a bar off Piccadilly; the one where, so many years later, I was to meet Mark.

'How do you like it in here then, Eddie?' Patrick had asked, after we had had a couple of beers. 'You'll get to learn a lot about life in here . . . Look over there,' he said, 'at those two fellas at the bar — to the right. Do you know what they are?'

'No. What?' I asked.

'They're rent,' he said, 'that's what.'

'They're *what*?' I asked, having forgotten our previous conversation about the subject.

'Rent. They're rent-boys,' he said. 'You can take them home with you, if you like. If you've got the money . . . They'll do anything.'

I looked at the two men — you could hardly call them boys — and thought how unsavoury they both looked; almost dangerous, like dark figures at the edge of some ugly, sinister painting.

'You don't fancy them — eh?' asked Patrick, making a joke of it.

At the same time, a group of stocky, middle-aged women marched up to the bar and ordered beers.

'You'd better not fancy that lot either,' Patrick said. 'They're lesbians.'

I remember how struck I was by the speed with which Patrick was able to name the sexual tastes of the bar's various customers. 'And that glamorous puss in the corner,' he added, 'the one with her legs crossed and who's puffin' away at a cigarette – she's no lady at *all*, Eddie. She's a man!'

That impressed me even more; for although I more or less stared at the woman in order to study her looks more closely, for me her deception was complete. I could see nothing about her to indicate that she was not a woman.

'You *sure*, Patrick?' I asked.

'Of *course* I am. I'm positive,' he said. 'Come on, Innocent, drink up – we'll have another.'

Patrick was the most wonderful company; and by then we'd been seeing each other quite a lot – usually on Sunday nights, after I'd had lunch with Len and Thelma – and I felt grateful towards him for his having taken me out so much, and for his having introduced me to city life, and to so many things that were new to me. And I can recall as well how that evening seemed suddenly to reach a climax after we had left the bar to go home, and had boarded a bus at Piccadilly and had climbed the stairs to the upper deck; only to find it full of chubby young women – girls, really; and none of them much older than myself; and all singing, at the top of their high-pitched voices, 'Maybe it's because I'm a lesbian, that I love London town.'

'Jesus!' said Patrick, 'look what we've landed ourselves with – *more* of them!'

'Don't you like them?' I asked, thinking how very cheerful they all seemed.

'Oh, it's not that,' he said, as he slipped an arm around my shoulders. 'It's not that I don't like them, Eddie. I don't give a damn what people do. It's just that I was thinking the upper deck would be empty, as it often is at this time of night, and that we could chat; which we can't do against this din, can we?' And it was as Patrick said this that I suddenly seemed to know how our evening was going to end, and I felt glad of it.

'I thought you liked girls,' I said to him, teasingly.

'I like anything,' he answered, squeezing my shoulder. '*Anything*. I like you, Eddie – do you know that? I like you a lot.'

When we got home, Patrick insisted that I went with him to his flat, and as we came in, I noticed how warm the room was and I guessed that he had left some form of heating on. There was a lamp switched on in a corner, making the room seem friendly and welcoming.

'Take your coat off,' Patrick said – a little sharply, I thought. 'I'll go to the john,' and off he went. 'Help yourself to a drink, Eddie,' he called out. 'You'd better not have whisky, though, or you'll be sozzled.'

I looked about me, and seeing a book on a table placed quite close to me, I picked it up. It was a collection of poems by Yeats – a writer I'd heard of, at least, but not yet read. And as I began thumbing through its pages, Patrick returned, having removed his shirt (which didn't surprise me at all) and looking dashingly athletic, I thought, in a white, ribbed, close-fitting vest.

'You know those poems?' he asked, as he came across to me and slipped an arm around my waist. 'Do you?' he asked again, as he took the book away from me and quickly brushed my cheek with his lips.

'Take this off – shall we, Eddie?' he said, as he swiftly unbuttoned my shirt. 'And these too?' he whispered softly in my ear, as he then began to unbuckle the belt of the soft cord trousers I was wearing.

And what I remember with such clarity is how sweet was the smell of his flesh. We had both been drinking quite heavily that evening, and it astonishes me to think

89

that the smell of beer and whisky didn't predominate. I just know that as he slipped out of his clothes and then came to stand in front of me naked, I have this memory of our sharing such a very particular bodily smell – good, clean; marvellously rich it was – and one that grew even stronger as he drew me down to lie with him on the carpet, before the soft glow of an electric fire; where he had hastily spread a rug to make us more comfortable. And I remember too how strangely beautiful I found his body – more muscular than I had expected it to be; and how I noticed a strong, blue vein that curled snake-like across his forearm and on towards his fingers.

'You like this, Eddie?' he asked, as he caught hold of one of my hands and guided it swiftly towards his groin, and as he then slipped one of his own hands between my legs and began to fondle my testicles.

'Yes,' I answered, because I did: because I found his penis strong and nicely formed, and because as he began to kiss me and so to heighten the emotion flowing between us, I knew that I wanted to give in – that I wanted him to make love to me, and to experience, which I had not done as yet, a different type of sex from the one that I had experienced with Tom in the woods; one that would make me richer, I thought, and wiser, and that might put me more at ease with myself.

'What do I do *here*, Eddie?' I heard Mark ask. 'Do I turn right or left?' – which brought me sharply back into the present. There was scarcely time for me to to recognise where we were, and to know which direction we had to take, before we arrived at a crossroads.

'Right, Mark!' I almost shouted, as a signpost loomed in front of us. 'We turn right! Here! Now!'

Mark had to make a sharp swerve, and there was a noisy screech of brakes as he just managed to swing the nose of the car into the narrow country lane that led to my aunt and uncle's farm. It was about to turn dark, and the car's headlamps had been switched on, and their harsh beams of light were raking the hedgerows at either side.

'What the heck do we do, Eddie,' Mark asked, sounding a little unnerved, 'if something comes the other way?'

'Don't worry,' I answered. 'People are used to the narrowness of the roads and lanes down here. They'll stop; and they'll reverse their car to some gateway where they can pull in. Or we'll do that, if one seems nearer – and then we'll pass each other carefully.'

Mark thought this quaint and rather amusing. 'So this is the country, is it?' he said, with a smile all over his face. 'Ha! you country lad, you,' he added with a laugh, forgetting, I thought, that I was a grown man. Then he leaned across and kissed me.

I had never imagined that I would be able to take someone with me into my past – not someone with whom I was intimate, in the way that I was with Mark. And had my parents still been alive, I know it couldn't have happened. So I felt particularly grateful towards my aunt Sarah for having said, when I had asked to bring Mark with me, 'Bring anyone you like, Eddie. You know you can. You are always welcome here.'

None the less, I did feel a trifle apprehensive as we arrived, worrying what my aunt and uncle would think of Mark and whether they would guess how close we were to each other; or whether I would need to give some hint of it perhaps, or some direct form of explanation. How stupid that proved to be, however, and how lacking in an understanding of people's characters; for no sooner had we brought our luggage in from the car than my uncle said to us, as if to put us more quickly at our ease, 'We've put you in the big room at the front, Eddie. You'll both be comfortable there . . . Apple sweet,' he added, with a smile.

'Yes,' said my aunt, chiming in. 'And Amy's been here today, giving a hand; so the bed's had a good airing. And there are clean towels on the rack, Eddie, beside the washstand; and – well, you know about the toilet, don't you? You'll have to explain that to Mark. It's a little primitive here, Mark, I'm afraid.'

'What did your aunt mean by that?' Mark asked as we made our way up the twisting wooden staircase that led to the upper floor.

'Oh, I'll explain . . . You'll see,' I answered, noticing that I was passing things on the walls that were familiar to me from my childhood. A pretty mirror, with a small, painted shelf beneath it, that I knew would become a treble looking-glass, if one released a small catch at its side. A large photograph of my aunt's parents – my grandparents – dressed soberly in black, and seated on heavy, country chairs before a whitewashed stone wall; with, placed next to it, a sepia-coloured photograph of my uncle Fred in uniform, looking terribly fit, I thought, and young; and with a mischievous twinkle in his eye.

'Your uncle?' Mark asked.

'Yes. In the army. Smart – wasn't he?'

'Sexy, too,' Mark answered. 'Do you think –?'

'No, I *don't*,' I said firmly, knowing Mark's tendency to believe that all men shared his sexual preferences.

'Well, they don't have children, do they?' he said.

'Lots of people don't have children,' I said, hoping to end the subject. 'Go through that door, Mark,' I added, 'straight ahead of us. Our room's beyond that.'

Mark pushed open the door of a bedroom that was never used – except perhaps at Christmas-time, when there might be a few card tables placed around the bed – and that more or less served as a corridor, leading to the much larger room beyond; where, as we went in, we were met by the delicious smell of apples and the comforting glow of a small coal fire burning in an open, cast-iron grate.

Mark sniffed the air, as if to say how puzzled he was by the smell.

'Look,' I said, crossing to lift a corner of the bed's thick coverlet, and to reveal on the floor beneath it a large wooden tray full of dark-green, sour-looking cooking apples.

'It's the best way to store them,' I explained. 'They're beneath all the beds. Each apple has to be placed free of the rest, so that if one happens to rot, the others won't be affected. Lovely smell, though – isn't it? "Apple sweet", as my uncle said.'

'And what about the toilet?' Mark asked. 'What do I need to know about that?'

'Well, there's no lavatory at this end of the house, so we'll have to use this,' I said, pointing to a heavy, walnut commode in one of the bedroom's corners.

'Use *that*!' Mark exclaimed with a laugh, as he lifted up its lid.

'Yes. *That*,' I answered him, in a slightly bossy manner.

The next morning – that was last Saturday morning – I woke early, with Mark sleeping beside me, and with the sun already up and casting sharp beams of light on to the room's faded Turkish carpet. Should I get out of bed, I wondered, and go down to breakfast without Mark? Or should I wait for him to wake? At which point I heard a gentle knock on the bedroom door.

'Come in,' I said quietly, so as not to wake Mark; and saw the door open and my uncle appear in a dressing gown, carrying a small tea-tray in his hands.

'Thought you'd like a cup of tea,' he said, placing the tray on a table beside me. 'Mark still asleep?' he asked.

'Sounds like it,' I replied – at which my uncle smiled. 'Well, come down when you're ready,' he said. 'You slept well, I hope.'

'Yes,' I answered. 'Very. Mark too, as you can see.'

I expected my uncle to leave the room, but instead he crossed to its main window, where he paused to look out.

'Your aunt and I are pleased you're here, Eddie,' he said. 'You know that, don't you?'

'Thanks, Uncle Fred,' I answered. 'Yes, I do.'

'I just wanted to tell you that,' he said. 'That's all. Wanted you to know that.' With which he thrust his hands into his dressing-gown pockets and turned to leave.

'Uncle Fred,' I said to him, 'Do you remember those Christmas parties? The ones you used to have when I was small?'

'Oh, my goodness me, yes. Wonderful times they were, weren't they? Up all night we used to be . . . Couldn't do that now, though, could we? . . . Still, they're there, you know, in memory – stored away. Everything's there. And it's wonderful to have it, too . . . *You* should feel that, Eddie, coming down here again, after so long.'

'I do,' I answered, as I heard the sound of dogs barking in the farmyard below the window.

'Ned's early,' my uncle remarked – Ned being one of the farmhands who worked for him. 'Thank God I don't have to do any of it now – not if I don't want to. But I still give a hand with the milking, you know. Machines now, of course, which makes it easier. And your aunt still bakes her own bread . . . Ah, well – life goes on. It has to . . . until you're in the grave,' he added with a rich chuckle and with a nod of his head towards Mark, as if to say that, in his view, the direction of my life might possibly lie with him. Then he quietly closed the door of the room and left.

VIII

TODAY IS A Sunday, and because it's been such a good one, I feel like writing about it now. As usual, I had lunch with Len and Thelma (what a habit that has become!), which was wonderful; and this evening I saw Mark, who has just left to go home because he has such an early start tomorrow; and he was wonderful too. What I enjoyed so much, though, was that Len came to collect me early. He usually comes at twelve and we eat at one, but today he arrived at eleven − deliberately, he said − so that we could have one of our talks, which I always enjoy − which we *both* enjoy. I know I have mentioned before how lucky I was to meet him, but I think I have not yet done his influence justice, for if Patrick educated me in the ways of the city, Len certainly did in the ways of the mind − in books, in literature, in thought.

We first met when I was only sixteen years old, and I am now in my thirties; and throughout all the years that we have known each other, he has always been my mentor, as I might call him − my spiritual guide. Not, as I have already said, that we are always in agreement regarding our tastes in *artistic* matters, but we are regarding politics, both of us being left-wing and, unlike Thelma, on the side of the poor and needy. In the world of books and words, though, there are differences over which we will often argue vehemently and occasionally almost quarrel.

Today, it's again been over my liking for the work of Ivy Compton-Burnett – *Dame* Ivy as we should call her, really, since she's been given that form of recognition. I tried to explain that it seems to me that she is portraying a subjective world in a surprisingly objective manner – something which I am sure must be difficult to do. Also, that, in my view, this seems to be a most serious aim for any modern writer; because it seems to be the inner world – the subjective one – that is causing us so much trouble today. Perhaps because it is being neglected, I said to him, due to so much emphasis having been placed upon the outer one and upon its scientific developments.

'It's like Hitchcock's films,' I told him, 'which you don't approve of either. You want everything to be rationalised, explained away; made logical . . .' And so it went on for almost an hour, Len answering me with *his* view, all of which was hugely enjoyable for us both.

Perhaps, too, I could have said (which I didn't think of doing at the time) that I see in Dame Ivy's work some of the family suffering that I myself have experienced – and that this probably draws me to it: that I've experienced tyranny and parental coldness and rejection, and awful physical humiliation. But, unlike the characters in Dame Ivy's novels, I've not stayed *within* the family and suffered it there. I've broken free – or I have *tried* to break free – and have attempted to face it on my own; something at which I've not been very successful, alas, in that I'm still somewhat inhibited – and, of course, still have the need at times to steal, which I am sure is a sign that I am running away from *something* – something inside myself; much as (as I have said before) that compulsion has slackened its grip on me a little since I've met Mark; and even more so, I've noticed, since I've talked to him about it.

What's been so encouraging has been to find that Mark can make jokes about it. 'You didn't nick anything, I hope,' he said playfully, when we left the farm after our weekend there. And I was able to laugh at that, rather than read it as being some kind of rebuke; and this has acted for me as a relief.

Regarding I.C.B. (Ivy Compton-Burnett): I wish I could have met her. She's now very old, and ill, I gather, according to something I read about her the other day; and it saddens me to think that, in a while, there will be no more of her books: no more of those cooped-up families of hers, who bicker and quarrel so, and who occasionally do quite murderous things to one another. But at least I'll have her novels in my bookcase − all of them − which I have collected gradually over the years. And I really do believe that if I *were* to become a writer I would use her work as some kind of model; in that she has shown such strength, it seems to me, in turning away from the topography of the outer world to create − well, I suppose one could say that her books are psychodramas of a kind, in the way that I suppose Jacobean plays might be said to be that. They recognise that the inner world is a dark and dangerous place, full of incestuous tendencies, in that all its 'characters' − all its various 'parts' − have no choice but to put up with the closeness of cohabitation. And there is no way out for them. They somehow have to get on with one another − with the mixtures of opposites they represent; otherwise, their world would split, become a divided one, and that would lead to their self-destruction. Which, now that I come to think of it, could surely be looked upon as being an apt or appropriate symbol of the present state of the world.

There! I've said something on paper that I've been wanting to say for a very long time; and even if it's been said clumsily, it is something I'm glad to have done. And perhaps tomorrow I'll be able to write about something else that I want to set down; a memory that came back to me only yesterday, but that I had obviously thrust out of my conscious mind for – how many years must it be? twenty or more? – and that has to do with that most difficult of all subjects (difficult for me, I mean), which is my relationship with my father.

It is unusual for me to want to write in the morning, before I go off to work. I write mostly in the evenings – sometimes quite late; or, at the weekends, during the afternoons, which is really my favourite time. But the memory I mentioned yesterday, that I seem to have kept locked away inside me in some private pocket of my unconscious, has been on my mind for the past half-hour, so I feel like trying to write about it now, while I am still in bed and when Mark isn't here.

It goes back to before my teens, when I must have been about ten, or maybe even younger; and to a Saturday afternoon when the house was quiet, with my mother having retreated to her room, and with Amy having cleared away the lunch things, and to my father calling me into his office, which, being placed at the very back of the house, and its windows heavily darkened by the tall yew trees of the churchyard, was always a rather gloomy place.

'Close the door, Edwin,' he said, in a voice that upset me, on account of the coldness of its expression.

'Come here,' he said, beckoning me towards his desk, and looking at me with those cold, reptilian eyes of his. 'Mr Barlow's been here,' he said, 'and has told me that you have taken something from his shop. A bag of sweets, apparently; when you thought he wasn't looking . . . Now, is this true, Edwin, or is it not?'

'It is, Father,' I answered – for, from the very first, if caught and questioned, I never denied my thefts.

'You mean, you did take them. You did steal them?'

'Yes, Father.'

'Why?' he asked, his voice almost quaking with suppressed anger. 'You must know it is *wrong* to take things that do not belong to you. So why did you do it? Your mother gives you pocket money – and surely enough for a bag of sweets. So why? Why did you do it?'

'I don't know, Father. I just did.'

'And that is all you have to say about it?'

'Yes, Father.'

There was a pause before he asked if I had done such a thing before.

'Yes, Father,' I said. 'Several times.'

I could see that he didn't want to believe me.

'You do realise how serious this is,' he said.

'Yes, Father. I think I do.'

'And what have you done with them – with the sweets? You can't have eaten them. Mr Barlow said this happened just now – just a short while ago. So where are they? What have you done with them?'

To this I refused to answer, and I knew at once that I was entering dangerous ground as far as my father's patience was concerned; but, without knowing why, I felt a strong need to defy him.

'Are you going to tell me, Edwin, where they are? Have you hidden them?'

I remember that I had in fact done just that. I hadn't opened the bag – I had just run with it to my room and hidden it beneath a pile of handkerchiefs in a drawer. For even in those early days of the compulsion from which I suffer, I wasn't interested in the sweets themselves. It was the act of taking them that meant so much to me; and the subsequent act of hiding them and of storing them away seemed part of some ritual I liked to enjoy; or perhaps needed to honour or to observe might be a better way of putting it.

'Come here,' my father said, stretching out to take hold of me and to draw me close to him. 'Stealing is *wrong*!' he said, with a sudden flash of anger, at the same time slapping me hard upon one of my thighs. 'Now – do you understand that, or not?'

I could feel the sharp tingle of his slap, and, in spite of being so young, can remember thinking to myself that it was probably going to hurt more in a while, once the initial shock of it had worn off.

'Do you understand?' he repeated, hitting me a second time. 'And tell me – will you? – now, what you have done with the *sweets*.'

Again I refused to answer.

'Undo your trousers,' my father then said. 'Unbutton them.'

This was the first time that my father had humiliated me in this way, and I recall how deeply shocked I was by it. But I was so in fear of him that I felt I had no choice but to obey, and I recall what a deep sense of shame I then experienced as I responded to his command.

'Now – push your trousers down,' he said – at which point I seemed to panic, because I recall that I let out a sharp scream: one of protest, I suppose, or simply one of defiance.

'Stop that, will you!' my father shouted at me. 'If you do things that are *wrong*, then you must be punished. It is time you learned that.'

I recall that I turned to glare at him, my eyes already wet with tears.

'Well, this will teach you,' he said, pushing me savagely across his knee and striking me upon the buttocks.

Again I screamed, and then sprang free of him, pulling my trousers up as I did so and racing into a corner of the room; from where I glared at him a second time.

'Do not look at me like that, Edwin,' he said. 'Just tell me what you have done with the sweets.'

'They're in a drawer,' I announced sullenly, tears now rolling down my cheeks, 'in my room; beneath some handkerchiefs.'

'*Which* drawer?' he answered sharply.

'One of the top ones: one of the small ones.'

'Right,' he said. 'Go and fetch them; and bring them *here* – to me.'

Again I glared at him, unable to believe that he was treating me in this way. But I then saw that I had to give in: saw that there was no concern, no kindness, in his eyes, and, because of it, ran obediently out of the room.

Why did my father treat me in that way, I wonder? Why was he so severe – so immediately judgmental? Knowing what I know about him now, was it because of his own unstable character, perhaps? Because beneath that veneer of orderliness and respectability there existed a wildness of spirit that couldn't easily be tamed? Obviously, it has to be something like that, for if he didn't rob people – didn't steal from them, in the way that I occasionally do myself – he certainly lived beyond his means. And also, it seems, to some extent on his wits, in that he had no regular job or form of steady work – no stable means of livelihood.

Whatever, I know that the pain he caused me runs deep, that his bouts of savagery, combined with the general coldness of his behaviour, is not something I care to dwell upon, even now. There must have been reasons for it, of course, but they aren't ones I can possibly guess at, since they probably lie in his early childhood; but I can't help thinking that, certainly in this respect, my upbringing could hardly be called a very normal one – if there is such a thing. To have had parents so set at a distance from each other, and to have had a father with such a suppressed but fiery temperament, does at least explain something about myself, and helps, I hope, to define a little of who I am.

IX

IT'S SUNDAY AGAIN, and at lunch today Thelma surprised Len and myself by saying that she had grown tired of the part-time job she has as a secretary at a school, and wanted to work full-time. Then she went on to say that what she would most like to do was to manage a restaurant.

I could see that Len was taken aback by Thelma's announcement.

'What restaurant?' he asked, a little sharply, I thought.

'Oh, a restaurant,' said Thelma, 'any restaurant. I've been looking at advertisements in the papers, and there are always jobs like that on offer.'

'But you've never wanted to come and work with me, have you? It would have helped at times, you know. So what's this all about? What's put this idea into your head?'

'Well, I thought I'd be good at it,' Thelma answered, with a quick toss of her head. 'Don't you think so, Eddie?' she said to me. 'Don't you think I'd be good at it?'

I didn't know quite how to reply to this; partly because I could see that Len wasn't pleased, and I didn't want to take sides. So I said only that I thought she might, as she is someone who likes people and who gets on with them.

'Well, there,' said Thelma, 'that's enough of a reason, isn't it? And I've never wanted to work at Battersea because you're there, Len – that's why. It's not always successful, you know, when couples work together.'

Len looked at her, trying to judge, I thought, whether she might be trying to get at him in order to draw him out; which she is inclined to do at times; but then quickly realised that it wasn't the case: that this was something she'd thought about, had made up her mind about and genuinely wanted to follow.

'There's nothing to keep me here, Len, is there?' she said. 'We've no children – no family. You're away a lot and come home late; and I'm bored – that's the main thing. And I don't think that is healthy, you know . . . On top of which,' she went on, 'I don't have Eddie's company so much these days, now that there's Mark . . . Do I, pet?' she said to me, with a smile that I was very glad of, since it was the first time that she had shown any sign of having accepted my new relationship.

'Well, we'll have to talk about it,' said Len. 'If it's something you *really* want to do, we'll talk about it – go towards it. But it is hard work, you know; and you do have trouble at times from some of the customers.'

'Oh, I'll soon sort *them* out,' said Thelma, with a laugh and a quick swing of her hips. '*Now*, which of you is going to make the coffee; because *I'm* not. Will you make it, Eddie dear? It's so good when you do. Len never makes it strong enough.'

Len looked at her suspiciously, wondering, no doubt, if her tease was going to develop into a more extensive one; but it didn't. 'You don't – do you, darling?' she added, with a warm, generous laugh; and going across to him, she gave him a quick affectionate kiss. 'And I make the worst bloody coffee of all three of us, so it's no use my doing it, is it?'

'I'll make it,' I said, getting up from the table. 'I'll make it, Thelma.' And I left to go into the kitchen, picturing as

I went how Thelma might look in charge of a restaurant, employing the sway of her personal charm, which was quite considerable; and being pleased to hear Len say to her, once I had gone, that the last thing he wanted was for her to be bored; that it was no good for either of them; but he spoke, I thought, with a touch of sadness in his voice; perhaps because he sensed that what Thelma really wanted was a family to look after, which was something she'd never had. Anyway, whether Thelma will ever achieve her aim remains to be seen. She might, because she does have a way of getting things done at times. On the other hand, she might not, because she is so often full of plans that do not come off, such as that she and Len should go on a cruise, or on holiday in Jamaica; but they usually end up doing neither, and the only type of break they seem to get is just a few days on the south coast – in Hastings, perhaps, or Brighton.

What a gap there has been since I last wrote in this book. Summer seems not only to have come but to have almost gone as well. For here we are, already close to the end of August, with the nights beginning to lengthen and the evenings at times a little cold. How very varied our climate is, for there can still be an Indian Summer, when, in September or October, the sunshine suddenly returns and the days are hot and golden. Right now, though, it's definitely a little on the chilly side, and you have to think about what to wear when you go out. Or certainly Mark and I experienced that last week when we went off for a few days – neither of us having had a summer holiday – and slept and lazed in a small guest-house close to the sea – near Aldeburgh, in Suffolk.

'Don't you wish we had money?' Mark asked one night after supper, as we lay on our beds with the window a little open; and with a sweet-smelling breeze passing through it into the room.

'Money?' I asked.

'Yes. So that we wouldn't have to put up with places like this, that have no bar? Wouldn't you like it if we could stay at some posh hotel in Venice, perhaps, or Rome?'

'Not really, Mark. I don't think I'm cut out for places like that. I don't think I could cope with them.'

'Of *course* you could,' he replied. 'Of course you could, Eddie. You deserve something better than this: better than one boiled egg for breakfast.'

'The breakfasts are quite *good*,' I answered. 'There's nothing wrong with them. And I quite like the owners – don't you? They seem decent enough.'

'I suppose so,' Mark answered, with a grunt. 'Come on, then – let's go for our walk. We'll see if there's a pub open somewhere, and have a beer.'

I've written this partly to get back into this notebook; which I find can act for me as a kind of lifeline, in that it helps to put order into things; and also to remind myself that I have now known Mark for quite some time – for several months – and that for me to have maintained such a close relationship for *that* length of time must count as quite an achievement. It's been mainly due to Mark's persistence, I have to admit, more than it has been to mine; due to his having had enough patience to put up with me and with my various faults and weaknesses. I have kept thinking that it will end – that I'll fail him in some way: perhaps by suffering some awful bout of introversion; or that I'll suddenly give in to my compulsion to steal and perhaps will finally be caught – and, well, punished, which is how I think of it, since that pattern is so ingrained in me. Yet the miracle has been that it hasn't happened and that we've managed to stick together, and have even drawn closer to each other as the days and weeks have gone by.

Perhaps it is the effect of this that has provoked an unusual confrontation of sorts: one that occurred only last night – after we had got back from our Suffolk holiday, and Mark had gone home to his flat and I had been about to go to bed. Perhaps the growing confidence I feel, due to the stability of our friendship, and also (I cannot discount this) to my having confronted my past such a lot during this last year (both outwardly and inwardly), provoked me into an action that I had not thought to take before; one that I took instinctively, without thought or premeditation of any kind – which was to go into my lumber room, as I call it, where the major part of my 'collection' is stored, switch on the light (which happens to be just one naked light-bulb that dangles from the ceiling), then lock myself in. Which seems a strange thing for me to have done, considering that I was alone and that it was late at night, and that there was no danger of anyone calling.

Why am I doing this? I remember asking myself, as I stared about the room, and at its stacks of shoe-boxes and old suitcases and the like, in which my trophies are neatly stored. I am doing something I have not really done before or ever felt a real *need* to do. It is true that I do keep the room locked; and it is true as well that Mark, and Thelma too, for that matter, have asked me several times what I keep in there; to which I have answered 'Oh, junk, mostly', or something like that.

'How *big* a room is it?' Mark asked me one day, to which I replied 'Smallish', which was rather vague. 'Big enough to be a bedroom?' he asked. 'Oh, no,' I said; which in fact was a lie, since the room would certainly take a single bed – perhaps even a narrow double one.

'You can see it if you want to, Mark.' I had then risked saying; to which he had answered, 'Oh, I believe you,

Eddie. I just thought how useful it would be if you had an extra room, and if we didn't have to sleep in here' – meaning in the living room – which fortunately ended our conversation.

However, there I was – alone; locked in with all my things – with all my secrets, as I suppose one might speak of them, since only I know of their existence, and of how, over so many years, they have been added to one by one. What on earth would someone else make of them? I thought, as I opened one of the shoe-boxes and looked at a neat collection of wallets, each with a small label – or card, rather – pushed into it, upon which was written a date, a place and a time. For if I have destroyed all evidence of their owners – such as their addresses and so forth, or, occasionally, a photograph – I have felt it necessary to keep a reminder of exactly where and when each of the objects was stolen. And this applies to *everything* – not just to the purses and wallets, but also to the books, the watches, and even the occasional article of clothing, which is not something I steal very often. Each of them bears one of these cards, either stuck or pinned on to them; or, in the case of the wallets, just slipped into them.

How on earth did I manage to do it? I found myself asking. And why? Why have I needed to behave in this eccentric, indeed criminal, way? My father was right, I thought. What I have done is *wrong*. Stealing really is a crime. And yet – well, it seems to be something that I have *had* to do; that my mind has compelled me to do; and against which, it would appear, I have had no means of defence.

I've kept thinking this morning about something that a character says in one of Ivy Compton-Burnett's novels, which is that she (the character is a woman who has stolen something either to help or please her husband) doesn't think that all crime is noble, much as she can forgive herself for what she has done. To which she adds, 'I am not a modern person.'

Well, unlike Dame Ivy's character, I am not sure that I can really forgive *myself* for having done what I have done; but I don't think that all crime is noble, either – or, indeed, that any form of it is: which makes me not a 'modern' person also, I suppose. Yet, if I am to be honest, I cannot truly say that I feel remorse. I did what I did. I do what I do – and for years I did it regularly. And there before me, in that room last night, I confronted – I came face to face with – the substance of all my 'crimes'; all neatly stored in their suitcases and their boxes; all recorded by the small notices that are attached to them. And there, for the moment at least, they will remain.

Will I ever find the strength, the power of will, to dispose of them, I wonder? Will I ever arrive at the point when I can invent some means, some method of interring them, and so of disposing of the evidence of my wrongdoing? Somehow, I doubt it. Even if the improvements that have been taking place of late continue. Even if Mark's good company and good influence, and his splendid generosity of spirit, help to dispel this obsessive compulsion from which I have always suffered, something tells me that I shall still have to keep – shall still have to guard – my secret hoard of mementoes; that in some peculiar way they act for me as a kind of anchor; as a kind of stabiliser for my life: that, odd though it may seem, the substantiality of their evidence is important to me; that it acts as a kind of repository in my mind, in which such a lot of me is contained and stored away; and that, curious though it may seem, it serves to support and sustain my identity.

Seventeen years ago (why I am now going back again in time I really don't know) when I was living in Battersea, in Rufus's flat, and working in Len's restaurant, I came home late one night to find Charlie stretched out, asleep, I thought, in one of the old armchairs in the living room, with two of Rufus's dogs curled up at his feet and one of the smaller ones on his lap. And because the night air was cold and one of the french windows was open, I crossed the room to close it.

'That you, Eddie?' Charlie muttered, obviously having heard me come in.

'Yes,' I said. 'I've just got back.'

'Ah,' he answered, as if he hadn't quite registered my words.

'I've closed the window, Charlie. It's cold.'

'You've what?'

'I've closed the window.'

'Ah . . . Lock it, then. The key's on a nail,' Charlie muttered, 'to the right of the window. Lock it, will you? There's a good lad.'

I found the key and used it.

'Isn't Rufus here?' I asked.

'No,' said Charlie, 'he bloody well isn't. Go to bed, Eddie. You need your sleep.'

'Well, aren't *you* going to bed, Charlie?' I said to him. 'You can't be comfortable in that chair.' And to my surprise, this provoked from him a sudden flash of anger. 'Do as I bloody well *tell* you, will you!' he more or less shouted at me, stirring in his chair and rolling his eyes in what I found a disturbing fashion.

'What you up to, Eddie – eh?' he then asked, in a very aggressive tone of voice. 'Why don't you mind your own bloody business?'

I thought it best not to reply to this and decided to leave the room quietly; but as I made a move to go, one of the dogs woke up, yawned, and pulled itself to its feet; then it came across to me and began brushing its nose against my ankles.

'Come *here*,' Charlie growled at the dog. 'Get *away* from him.'

The dog turned and looked at Charlie, as if to question what he had said.

'Come *here*, you bastard,' Charlie repeated, with a touch of wildness in his voice – which made the dog quickly obey and allowed me to sneak out of the room.

There were few lights on in the flat. None in the passage that led to the bedrooms and just one left on in the kitchen, which drew me towards it, half thinking that I could do with a drink before I turned in, and that I could clean my teeth there as well. But before I had reached the kitchen door, Charlie burst out of the living room into the passage, and began shouting at me again.

'What you fucking well *up* to, Eddie – eh?' he asked.

'I'm going to get a drink, Charlie, and to clean my teeth.'

'Clean your fucking *teeth*!' he said. 'What the hell for?'

'Because I always clean them, Charlie – that's why – before going to bed. And I want to get a drink as well.'

'You want a *drink*!' he shouted, with a nasty snarl. 'You want a bloody *drink*?'

'Yes,' I answered, 'I *always* have one.'

'Well, come here, then,' he said, 'and have a swig of *this*.' And he raised a beer bottle that he held in one of his hands. '*That's* what you need, Eddie, you little bastard, you.'

I had no idea why Charlie was behaving in this way. Odd though he was, he had always been a rather gentle, docile character, so his behaviour startled me and I hastily backed away.

'What you up to, Eddie – eh?' he said yet again, scowling at me and taking a single step towards me.

'I don't know what you're talking about, Charlie,' I said. 'I'm not up to *anything*!'

'Oh, yes, you are, you little monkey, you . . . come here! I'll *teach* you!'

By this time his behaviour had become quite frightening and I recall wondering what I should do – whether I should run into the kitchen, perhaps, or even escape through the main entrance-door of the flat, which was immediately behind me – when I heard the sound of Rufus's van turning into the driveway from the street.

'That's Rufus,' I said to Charlie.

'That's *who*?' he growled.

'It's Rufus, Charlie. He's just driven into the drive-way.'

Charlie listened, and obviously realised that this was so; then, to my surprise, he turned and went back into the living room, muttering, 'Little monkey, you are, Eddie,' as he went. At the same time, Rufus let himself in through the door behind me.

'Hello, Eddie,' Rufus said, in a very cheerful tone of voice. 'What are *you* doing here? On your way to bed?'

'No – not yet,' I answered. 'I was about to clean my teeth and make myself a nightcap.'

'Where's Charlie?' Rufus asked.

'He's in the living room.'

'He all right?'

'Yes. Why?'

'Oh, nothing,' said Rufus. 'I thought he might have been drinking.'

For some reason I didn't tell Rufus that he had been, or indicate to him that Charlie had been unpleasant to me. I simply said, 'He was asleep when I came in, Rufus. A window was open, so I closed it.'

'Good lad,' said Rufus, passing me and heading down the passage towards the living room. 'You're a good lad, Eddie,' he repeated, patting me affectionately upon the shoulder, 'one of the best.'

Writing about it now, I realise that it was probably this irrational exchange with Charlie that made me decide to leave Rufus's flat and, with Len's help, to move to a place of my own. For, after it, I never felt quite comfortable there again, even though there was no repetition of Charlie's aggressiveness and he returned to being the gentle, docile creature I had always taken him to be. Nor did he show any sign of embarrassment about it, neither later that night, as he went to bed, nor at breakfast the following morning. And I was unable to understand what the cause of his turbulence had been. I just know that from that night on, I behaved a little differently in the flat, keeping more to myself and seeing a little less of my two flatmates. They didn't appear to notice it, however, and certainly neither of them commented in any way upon the change in my behaviour. Obviously, in their eyes, things were as normal between us. Finally, when I left, Charlie twice raced into the garden to blow a sharp blast upon his whistle (which, I imagined, might have been a protest against my leaving, because I am sure that he was fond of me and enjoyed having me there), but I noticed an odd look in his eye that seemed to reflect the wildness of his expression when he had turned on me that night. Yet, until that moment, the general air of normality had remained – and, as I have said before, odd trio that we were, or that we appeared to be, we were happy enough together.

X

HOW CIRCULAR LIFE seems to be, with memory ever at work, bringing the past back into the present. I experienced this today on receiving a letter from my aunt, inviting Mark and I to go down to the country again. For as I was reading it, I suddenly remembered, as if it had occurred just a few days ago, an incident I had forgotten, or perhaps had forced out of my mind. It was connected with Mark having asked me, when we had stayed with my aunt and uncle earlier in the year, if we could see my parents' house.

'Where you were born, Eddie,' he said. 'You speak about it a lot.'

'Do I?' I answered, not being conscious that this was so.

'Yes. You do. You're always going back to it. Always saying *something* about it. Don't you think it would be good for us to see it together?'

I panicked when he said this, and quickly hid what I was feeling by muttering that I didn't think that we could.

'Why?' Mark asked – a little bluntly, I thought.

'Well, because it's sold – that's why. The house has been sold, Mark.'

'So what? We can see it from the outside, can't we? There's nothing to stop us from doing that.'

'No, there isn't,' I answered, but showing by the tone of my voice that I wasn't too keen on the idea.

'What is it, Eddie?' Mark asked. 'Have I done something wrong? Don't you *want* us to go there? Or is it that *you* don't want to go there, perhaps?'

'I'm not sure,' I answered truthfully, because I realised how confused my feelings had become. 'I don't know, Mark. But we will go, if you really want us to.'

'Look, Eddie, I don't want to —'

'I know you don't. I was just caught out — that's all. Listen, it's not far. The town's only two miles away, so why don't we do it now, before lunch. It's Saturday. The square will be busy. We can park behind the church, then walk from there through the churchyard.'

And that is what we did. We drove along the winding country road where I had walked so often as a boy, entered the town from the north, then parked the car behind the church, where I knew there was always plenty of room.

As Mark locked the doors of the car he looked across at me apprehensively.

'Are you all right, Eddie?' he asked. 'Are you sure you want us to do this?'

'Yes,' I answered, doing my best to sound positive about our decision.

'Right,' Mark answered with a nod. 'Let's go then, shall we?'

Without speaking, I left the car to join him; then led us quickly around to the front of the church, where the churchyard's yew-lined pathway led forward in a straight line towards a side entrance to the town's square, which we could see was already busy with cars and many shoppers.

'There it is,' I suddenly said to Mark — meaning the house; and speaking in a half whisper, almost as if we were stalking it.

'Where?' Mark asked, also lowering his voice.

'To the right. Between the trees. We can see the back of it. The landing window.'

'Looks a bloody gloomy place to me,' said Mark. 'No wonder you didn't like it.'

'But that's just the back of it,' I answered, surprising myself by being defensive about the house. 'You'll see. It looks different from the front.'

Again the two of us fell into silence as we made our way along. Then, as we finally reached the narrow flight of steps that marked the path's end, I stopped and turned to look back; feeling a need to see the view from there of the church tower.

How often have I watched it soar upwards as it did then; its stonework a mixture of pinks and greys set against the soft light blue of the sky. It will always be there, I thought, both in my mind and in reality. And it will be there too when I am no longer here on this earth, with generations ahead of me looking up as I did then, towards the church tower's gilded weathercock turning cheerfully in the breeze. Already my parents had come and gone, and I knew that, before I reached old age, I would be joining them.

'How *can* you know that?' Mark had asked me one day, when I told him about this premonition that I have had since I was small.

'I don't know,' I had answered. 'There are some things that you just do. I don't mean that I'm going to die soon, Mark – don't worry. But I know that I won't see seventy. Sixty, perhaps, but not seventy.'

'Rubbish!' Mark had replied to this. 'You do talk rot at times, Eddie – honestly you do.'

I had laughed at this, much as I thought it might be true. 'Well, I'm here now, at least,' I'd said to him.

'Thank God for that,' he'd answered, giving me a hug.

As we entered the square, I told Mark that we would

be able to see the house towards the right, which meant that we both saw it at the same time – and both stopped walking as we confronted it.

How different it seemed from how I'd remembered it. It was as if it had been robbed of all its darkness – all its shadow; and now seemed like the other houses surrounding it – a rather simple, almost innocent, abode.

'That it?' Mark asked, knowing that it was.

'Yes,' I answered, and we began to move on.

'It's being done up,' Mark commented, as we drew closer and saw a step-ladder in one of the ground-floor rooms, where someone – a painter or a plasterer – was at work.

'Yes – well, it's sold,' I said, as Mark strode quickly across the pavement and pressed his face against one of the windows – causing the workman to pause in what he was doing and to look down at him.

'Good morning,' Mark called out. 'Doing the place up, I see.'

'Yes.' The man answered good-humouredly, in the way that country people so often do. 'It needed it too. We're decorating the whole place – outside and in.'

'Do you mind if we come in?' Mark asked. 'Take a look at it? This friend of mine was born here. In this house, I mean. Grew up in it.'

The workman came down from his ladder, then crossed the room to push up the lower half of the sash window.

'You Mr Carpenter's son, then?' he asked, staring at me. I nodded.

'Well I'll be blowed. I knew your father, I did. Used to have a drink with him at times – over there: at the Castle. You're –'

'I'm Edwin,' I answered. 'Carpenter.'

'That's right. You went off or something – didn't you? – for some reason. Left home.'

'Look,' said Mark, quickly interrupting, and knowing it was wise to do so. 'Do you mind if we take a quick look round? Just a few minutes. Just to – well –'

''Course you can. If that gentleman's Mr Carpenter's son, you're more than welcome to do so . . . The door isn't locked, in any case. Just give it a push. It's Saturday. There's no one here but me . . . Yes, take a look round – do. Just come and tell me when you leave.'

The speed of Mark's action had unsettled me, and I half wanted not to enter the house; but Mark more or less pushed me through the door, knowing instinctively, I guess, that the experience was going to be good for us.

'Shall we go upstairs?' he asked. 'Shall we do that first?'

I nodded yes to this, and we swiftly made our way up to the first-floor landing.

'Big room,' said Mark, as he pushed open the door of what had been our sitting room. 'Good view of the square, too,' he added, as he crossed towards the room's two windows.

'That clock right?' he asked, pointing towards the neatly proportioned clock tower that perched on the roof of the town hall.

'Usually,' I answered, recalling the night when I left home, when I had nervously read its time.

'You'd hardly *need* a clock in *this* house – would you?' said Mark with a laugh; to which I had nothing to say in reply because I was feeling too emotional to speak; with so many memories suddenly flooding back to me; and hearing, as I did, the delicate sound of my mother's laugh, and the much heartier one of Amy; and seeing, in my mind's eye, the sight, so awesome, of my father when he was dying; looking at me in such an impersonal way, then turning on to his side to stare at the bedroom wall.

'Now,' said Mark, 'which was your room, Eddie? Which was *your* bedroom?'

Our tour of the house didn't last long. All the rooms were empty; some of them stripped of their wall coverings; the kitchen not at all as I had remembered it, with brand-new cabinets and fitted cupboards, and a pale-green Aga cooker where Amy's old black range had been. So there was little to look at. No furniture, no pictures, no books. And apart from the sudden flush of memories that had come back to me in the sitting room, when Mark had spoken about the clock, I experienced few remembrances of things past. Even my father's study, which was what I had most feared seeing, just looked like a 'room' – any room: bare; empty; and not at all gloomy in the way that I had remembered it. This was partly, I have to say, because one of the churchyard's yew trees had been felled, which had lightened the room considerably. All of which made me reflect upon the fact that the past exists solely in memory; that its reality is a totally subjective one; and that attempts to capture it through exterior things are inevitably likely to flounder, as this one did that day.

'Bring it all back to you?' asked Mark, as we left the house and began walking back to the car.

'Funnily enough, no,' I answered with a laugh. 'Not really, Mark. A few things; but not much, really.'

'Well, at least it's made you cheerful; so it must have been good for you in *some* way or another – good for us both . . . Shall we do the church while we're here?' he then suggested. 'Almost a grand building, isn't it? Did you have to come here for services when you were small? A lot, I mean?'

'Oh, yes,' I answered, seeing myself accompanying my mother almost every Sunday, and hearing the relentless toll of the church bell as it called the congregation to prayers. I recalled too the deep sense of quietude there always was on that day, seeming to unite the town with the fields and moorland surrounding it. This memory was now mixed in my mind with that of the smells issuing from doorways or kitchen windows, where a Sunday roast was being prepared; or, as far as the poor were concerned, that were issuing from large roasting pans that were being brought home from the local bakery – where, for just a few pence, use had been made of the oven.

'Smells of wax,' said Mark, smiling at me. 'And of Brasso too,' he added, as he pushed open the church door and ushered me inside.

Thelma 'dropped in' to see me today. For once, she had done what she had *said* she would do yesterday (which was Sunday) when Mark and I (yes, *Mark* and I) were having lunch with her and Len.

'We don't see much of each other these days, do we, pet?' was how she began our conversation, once she had settled herself upon the sofa. 'Not now there's Mark,' she added; but not said, I am glad to be able to write, with any hint of reproachfulness in her voice.

'And that's how it should be,' she went on. 'It'll force me to do something more with my life. Go out. Get more work. Try that restaurant idea of mine. You did mean it, didn't you, Eddie, when you said that I was good with people?'

'Of course I did,' I answered. 'You *are*, Thelma.'

'Well, it's nice of you to say so, sweetie,' she replied; somewhat nervously, I thought, and I noticed that her lips had begun to quiver.

'Thelma! What's wrong?' I exclaimed.

'Oh, nothing, pet. Nothing serious. It's just that – well, I'm not always as confident as I look, you know. I often say big things – such as that I'd like to run a restaurant on my own, but when it comes to it, it's a different story.'

'No it isn't,' I said, trying to help her to be positive. 'Or it doesn't *have* to be.'

'A lot of the trouble is that I'm a woman,' she continued. 'I try at times to think and behave like a man, but I'm *not* that, am I? That's mainly why it's so difficult, Eddie. And I can't talk to Len about it, either.'

'Why ever not?' I asked.

'I don't know. I just can't. Perhaps I'm too proud. Perhaps I don't want him to know that I am afraid: don't want him to see that side of myself. I'm sure that's wrong of me, because I'm sort of hiding myself from him – disguising myself; but there – I can't.'

'Which is why you're talking to me about it. Is that what you're saying?'

'I suppose so, sweetheart,' she answered, taking out a handkerchief and quickly wiping away a tear that had fallen on one of her cheeks. 'Yes, I suppose it is. It's good to talk to someone about it.'

'But perhaps the truth is that you don't really *want* a heavier job, Thelma – a full-time one. Perhaps you are forcing something.'

'No. I am not,' she answered, looking directly at me. 'I know I'm not.'

'And it isn't that you're wanting to compete with Len, Thelma – is it? That you're wanting to do what he does?'

'I've thought about that,' she replied. 'Wondered if it might be so; but I'm sure it isn't. If it was, it wouldn't be good, would it? Wouldn't be right . . . No, I *do* have to make more use of myself: be more active. I dread the idea of becoming like my mother; sitting at home all day and getting to be the size that she became as she grew older: stuffing herself with food because she was bored. I'm fat enough as it is.'

'You're big, Thelma, but not fat,' I said to her, even though it wasn't entirely true.

'You're being kind, Eddie. I'm already a lot overweight. And the thought of my becoming like my mother really frightens me . . . I remember once, when I was in my teens, how she called me into her bedroom and asked me to unlace the stiff-boned corsets she always wore. Pink ones they were, that held her together, and that she had to have made for her. And I remember too how I could hardly bring myself to do it, fond of her though I was . . . No. I *need* to be active, Eddie,' she said. 'I *need* to do more. There are some women who don't mind being at home – don't mind being indoors and having their menfolk go out – but *I'm* not one of them. For one thing, I'm no good at domestic things, as you well know. I simply am not.'

'Then how can I help you? You're my best friend, Thelma. You always have been. So what can I do to help?'

'What you're doing now, pet. Letting me spill a bit, so that I don't boil over. Letting me just talk and being a good listener – which is what you always are. Do you know that? A really good one. And there aren't many of those.'

'Well, if that's all I have to do, it isn't difficult,' I answered. 'Look – let's go out, shall we? Go to Mark's place – in Fulham. Have a few drinks . . . We don't go out together very often these days. Wouldn't it be nice; fun; wouldn't it be good for us?'

'Oh, I don't think I can do that, Eddie,' she said. 'I don't drink a lot, and – well – there's Mark. I'm not sure that he likes me.'

'Thelma! Whatever makes you think that?'

'I just do. I always have done. Ever since we first met.'

'Well, perhaps that's because you were nervous of him, Thelma; and perhaps he was nervous of you. After all, it's quite new for me to have a friend – to have found someone I really like at last.'

'Perhaps,' she answered, but she refused to go out;

and we just sat there talking and drinking coffee until midnight.

The nights are getting longer. Autumn is here already, and in the parks and gardens of the city the first dead leaves are now fluttering down from the trees. What a year it has been! A year of the old and the new, it could be called, I suppose. The new being my having met Mark and his having so quickly become such a part of my life, and the old, the excursions I have made into the past that have stirred up so many memories.

In those narrow country lanes, where I walked so often as a child, the winter berries will have already formed; grey-green at first, now touched by reds and golds. And in the coarse bracken close to the moors, the fruits of the wild blackberry bush will now be soft and sweet – ripe, and ready for picking. Soon, too, once the corn has been cut and its grain been stored, and once its straw has been bundled for winter bedding, the time of the Harvest Festival will begin. Huge loaves will be baked – some in the form of fan-shaped sheaves of wheat – ready to be placed upon the windowsills or before the altars of the area's small stone churches.

I can see it – hear it all – so clearly. The parson shuffling his way towards the pulpit, as the congregation sits, then coughs, then settles in the pews; with the white surplice of his robes dangling across the pulpit's edge, and mingling with the mixture of fruit and flowers that adorn it – and for which he and his congregation are now about to give thanks.

'All is safely gathered in', the choir will assert (defiantly, I used to think), before the 'winter storms begin'. Or it will be, 'We plough the fields and scatter the good seed on the land'. Which we do, of course; but we sow the seeds of our life without much thought, it seems to me, casting them here and there in our early years, with no mind as to whether they might fall upon stony ground or not. Then, with time, they grow – or some of them do.

For me, I know that when I was young and still in my teens, and when I was deciding that I would leave home, I was certainly casting seeds upon new ground, hoping to free myself from things that were cluttering me and were inhibiting my life. And I believed that what I was doing was right; that it was an action I had to take, or that I was meant to take. Yet for all the dramatics of that act, the rewards reaped have hardly been spectacular. After all, what am I? What have I become? A clerk – just that – working in a small South Kensington office. That is all. I've not been to college, for instance, or university. Not furthered myself in that respect. I have learned a lot through Len, it is true; and I have grown to love books and words – and paintings as well. But it's no great achievement, not when I think of what others do with their lives.

There is Mark – yes. At least there I have managed to find someone I really like at last; perhaps even love – and that's important, of course, as it would be to any-one, whatever their sexual tastes and prejudices. To have someone close to you *is* important; it helps to put meaning into your life. But on the other hand – seeing the more negative side of things – I still haven't given up stealing. The compulsive need to acquire things that do not belong to me still bothers me at times; much as I have been able to restrain myself of late and have somehow held it in check.

So, in a way, you could say that, from a sociological point of view, I am not a very nice person. I'm certainly not doing much for the world – that's for sure, in that I am not doing much for others. Just seeing to myself – that's all. Just making sure that I don't hurt anyone too much. Just doing my best to find out a little of who exactly

I am. However, I do have a right to take some pride in that, I guess, since I am struggling to be honest, at least. A muted life mine might be, and perhaps a rather shaded one as well, in that my stealing is kept secret. But it is a 'real' life, none the less, in that I accept its limitations, and that I do my best to honour them and to live within their bounds.

Ivy Compton-Burnett has died. I heard the news a few weeks ago on the radio and it surprised me; then I saw the obituaries in the newspapers. And soon, in a week or so's time, there is to be a memorial evening for her here in Chelsea – at Crosby Hall, which is just a short walk from where I live.

I told Len that I'd like to go to it, since I've been an admirer of her writing for so long, and the evening is open to anyone. But I can't think what form the evening will take, since it's not to be a religious service of any kind. There'll be no priest, apparently; none of religion's mumbo-jumbo; Dame Ivy having been an atheist, of course, and having had little time for religion; or for the Church and for its dogmas.

So I think I'll go. Just for the experience. And if I do, then perhaps I shall write a few words about it here – in this journal.

XI

THIS MORNING, I stole something – a wallet. It is the first time this has happened since I met Mark, and I felt doubly upset on account of that. I kept branding myself as a villain and a weakling – which, I kept telling myself, is what I am; when I thought of the upset it must have caused – meaning, for the person from whom I had stolen the wallet; even though it contained only a relatively small amount of money, a few business cards and a photograph of a child.

It *is* weak. It *is* villainous of me to have done this, I kept telling myself all morning – and there *is* no excuse for it. My better self does *know* that it's wrong; that crime is not noble; that it's a destructive, negative action; that it's the opposite of giving: the opposite of loving.

So I made up my mind then and there that I would speak about it to Mark, and so expose myself for once; even though the idea of my doing this daunted me – particularly because it had to be done at lunchtime, when Mark and I had arranged to meet in a bar.

'Where?' was his immediate reaction. 'Where did this happen?'

'On my way to work,' I answered with my head lowered. 'In a newsagent's, where I had gone to buy a paper. The man had decided to pay with coins, and had left the wallet on the counter, and I – well, I just took it.'

'Right,' said Mark, 'we're going there.'

'We're *what*?' I almost screamed at him, suddenly feeling frightened.

'We're going there: to the shop: to the newsagent's. We're going to say we've found the wallet in the street, and are wondering if some customer has lost it.'

'But they *know* me!' I said. 'I go there often. They'll remember that I was there this morning. They'll think it was me.'

'Well, it *was* you,' Mark answered, sharply. 'So the thing to do is to take it back.'

'And say I *took* it?'

'No, of course not, stupid. Just say you found it in the street – as I said.'

'As if they'll believe that.'

'Look,' said Mark. 'They'll be glad that someone's brought it back. They won't have ideas of that kind. You'll *seem* to be honest – that's the main thing.'

'No, Mark,' I answered, 'I don't want to do it.'

'Then I'll do it,' he replied. 'I'll take it back. I'll say I found it nearby. I'll say –'

'Mark, please,' I answered him, now almost white with fright at the idea, since it was the first time that I had even thought of returning an object that I had stolen – or, more accurately, that someone had suggested to me that I should.

Mark then ordered me (there is no other word to describe it) to look at him. 'Straight in the eye,' he said . . . 'Now,' he continued, once I had done what he had asked, 'are you going to do this, Edwin, or not? If I come with you? Or are you going to force me to do it for you?'

I knew we had reached a kind of climax – a clash of wills that had to be faced. And I knew as well, by the way that he had looked at me, that Mark was making a real test of it: that if I said no he would feel let down; feel that, after having confided in him – having almost asked him to help me put things right – I lacked the courage to follow my action through. So I said nothing. Just waited; almost watching myself, until the knowledge of what I *could* do – not what I must do – came to me.

'Well?' said Mark – not pressingly, but in a very quiet, very patient manner.

I looked at him and at his squarish, well-shaped head; at the neat cut of his hair and at his steady, dark-brown eyes; and saw there a being whom I valued; one who meant more to me at that moment than any other in my life.

'Well?' Mark repeated, in the same steady, quiet voice.

'I'll do it, but I don't want you to come with me . . . Now,' I said. 'I'll do it now, before I go back to work.'

'You sure?' Mark asked, wondering if I was seeking to get out of it, I thought.

'I'm sure,' I said. 'I'll do it now.'

And I did. I walked back to the shop, went straight into it, then asked the man behind its counter whether, by any chance, a customer of his had lost a wallet.

'Why?' he asked. 'Have you found one?'

'Yes,' I said, and took the wallet out of my pocket.

The man looked at me in what I took to be a question-ing way, then suddenly ducked his head and muttered, 'Just a moment, sir. I'll ask my brother,' and he disap-peared into the back of the shop, only to return almost immediately with the man who had served me earlier in the day.

'Yes?' the man said, screwing up his nose and look-ing across at me from behind half-moon, wire-rimmed spectacles.

'A wallet,' I replied, trying not to seem nervous. 'I was wondering if one of your customers has lost one. This one,' I said. 'I found it in the street – just a few yards away – and was about to take it to the police.'

The man took the wallet from me.

'Do you mind if I look inside it?' he then asked, which at first puzzled me.

'Of course not.' I replied. 'There's some money – a few notes; a photograph; a few business cards.'

'Well – yes,' he said, as he examined the wallet and drew out of it one of its owner's business cards: 'This is someone who calls here most days. I recognise the name. And he was here this morning. But he didn't say he had lost anything. He paid with change from his pocket, as I recall.'

'Perhaps you could ring him,' I said, 'since he's a customer of yours. It has to be his – doesn't it?'

I began to fear that he might suggest my taking the wallet to the police, which is what I dreaded the most.

'Oh, well – that's a good idea. Just hang on, will you?' he answered with a broad smile.

The man disappeared into the back of the shop again and his brother looked at me and nodded. Then other customers came in and he began to serve them.

I don't know whether I nodded back to him or not. I don't think that I did. I think that I just stood there somewhat rigid, cut off from what was happening; which I can now see was probably a form of self-protection. What I do recall is studying the shelves behind the shop's counter, and registering the various brand-names of the cigarettes on display. Also, that there was a neat stack of Swan Vestas matches, as well as a few small boxes of snuff.

'He hadn't even missed it!' the man who had made the telephone call cried out to me as he returned. 'He's really pleased: says how can he thank you?'

'I don't need thanks,' I said, feeling relieved. 'I just –
well, just wanted to make sure it had found its owner,
that's all. And it has.'

'Well, it's very good of you. Very kind of you, Mr –?'

'Carpenter,' I said.

'Sorry – I didn't know your name,' the man answered.
'We don't know the names of many of our customers, I'm
afraid. Or, if we do, it's just their first names – Bill, or
whatever.'

'Well, all's well that ends well,' I said; a little stupidly,
I thought, since it was so out of character for me to speak
in that way.

'It certainly *is*,' the man replied with a grin. 'Pity there
aren't more like you around, Mr Carpenter. With money
in it – notes – most people would just take it for themselves
and throw the wallet away.'

'Gracious me!' I exclaimed, or something of that kind;
and, with a nod of goodbye to his brother, I shook his hand
and left. I didn't feel at all proud of what I had done, but
just glad that it had been done with comparative ease. I
felt too that this act had meant a huge change in my life:
that I had relieved myself of some of the darkness with
which I was burdened. At the same time, though, I was
aware that, without Mark having prompted me into it, it
was something that couldn't have happened. It was his will
that had swayed mine; I had allowed it to guide and govern
my action; and because of that, I felt only little in the way
of what one might call any moral form of improvement.

Still, it was *something*, at least: something different; a new
twist in the way things happen. And I have to confess that
this evening when I came home, and before I began making
this entry in my journal, I did allow myself to picture for a
brief moment the deep look of pleasure there must have
been on the face of the owner of the wallet, when, out
of the blue, so to speak, he had learned by way of the

telephone not only that he had lost something he no doubt valued, but also that it had been found and was now being returned to him.

Tonight, I have been to the memorial evening in honour of the late Ivy Compton-Burnett, whose work I have admired for so many years and over which I have so often quarrelled with my friend Len. It was held in Crosby Hall, where I said it would be earlier; which is just a few streets away from my flat, and which more or less overlooks the river.

This was a new thing for me to have done, in that I am not accustomed to literary gatherings of that kind. So I deliberately went early, and was one of the first 'mourners' – must I call them that? – to arrive. Which allowed me to tuck myself away at the very back of the hall, where I was sure that no one would notice me. A few of the organisers of the event were already there, but they only glanced at me as I came in – merely checking, I thought, to make sure that I was no one they ought to greet – which made me feel comfortable. What a wonderful thing it was, though, I recall thinking, that this event should be taking place: that people should be gathering here from all over London – and, as far as I knew, from many other places as well – in order to pay their respects to a famous novelist. She wrote nineteen novels in all – I do know that – with the last one yet to be published; and all much in the same style, with few passages of description in them, and composed mostly of dialogue and conversation. And as I sat there, waiting for the evening to begin, I suddenly heard some of Dame Ivy's characters speaking, and it made me laugh. Not out loud, of course, but inwardly; because there is such a deep vein of humour running through all that she writes – or that she wrote, rather, since she is now with us no longer. And I found myself thinking of the various titles of her books: of *Brothers and Sisters*, of *Manservant and*

Maidservant, of *More Women than Men*; and remembering what a particular style of writing she achieved, and of how little her work depended upon the outside world and its depiction. She can never be really popular, I thought, because to read one of her books requires effort; but then, doesn't anything that is worthwhile need that? And aren't the rewards almost greater on account of it?

My ruminating in this fashion had made me forget where I was, and it was only the sudden awareness that the seats surrounding me were now occupied that drew me back towards the evening and to the purpose of my being there in that hall – which was soon quite full; and with everyone being rather quiet and reverential; and not dissimilar, I thought, to a congregation in church.

That effect didn't last long, however; for as the evening progressed, and as people were asked to stand up and to say whatever they wished about Dame Ivy – those who had known her, that is – the occasion took on the character not of a church service, or of a religious service of any kind. It became instead something much closer to that of a party. And what was so very moving was that the entire spirit of the evening sprang from the character of the deceased; from her many eccentricities; from the stories told about her famous 'teas', which used to be held in the flat she shared in Kensington with her friend Margaret Jourdain; from the one about the curious habit she had of at times thrusting a hand beneath the skirt of her dress in order to withdraw from it a handkerchief; kept, apparently, in a pocket in her underwear. And from one story (related in a letter that was read aloud and that had been sent by someone in the States) about her relationship with T. S. Eliot – the poet – and about how they tended to discuss not art and literature when they met, as one might have expected them to do, but their local butcher and baker and the price of Brussels sprouts!

How full of warmth the evening was. How full of deep fondness and affection. I felt very honoured and privileged to be present; and envious of the many people there who had known the author in person. Yet, at the same time, the wonderful, the most magical, thing was that, by the time the evening drew to a close, I felt as if she was more than familiar to me and had almost been a friend.

When I left the hall, I crossed the road to the Embankment, to where the moonlit waters of the Thames slipped gracefully beneath the Albert Bridge and towards other, more famous landmarks of the city – the Houses of Parliament, Big Ben, St Paul's – and eventually towards Greenwich. How extraordinary, I thought, as I leaned upon the Embankment's parapet, watching the lazy flow of the river's current encountering a small flotilla of barges that clung together in shadow and rocked gently to and fro, that the spirit should have such power: that it should be able to triumph, as it had been able to do that night, not just over the death of one particular person but over all things temporal and physical. For as I then turned and began to make my way home, and as I saw on the opposite side of the road many of the people who had attended the evening still standing about in groups – still chattering, still reminiscing, no doubt – I realised that there is nothing stronger in life than meaning, and that immortality, if there should be such a thing, is what we all aspire to achieve. Few of us will achieve it, alas – even in the smallest way. But I knew, as I looked up at the night sky and saw its sprinkling of silver stars, that this was true. Then I laughed out loud (which was a rather rare thing for me to have done) at the thought of Dame Ivy going to see a play by Samuel Beckett that was being performed at the Royal Court (the theatre in Sloane Square), and of how she had turned to say of its audience: 'How wonderful to be so intellectual'!

★   ★   ★

Thinking of it now, it seems to me that one of the saddest things about my childhood was that I never asked any of my schoolfriends home to have tea with me, which was something Amy was always encouraging me to do.

'You go to *their* houses at times,' I can hear her say, 'so wouldn't it be nice to have some of them here? . . . You know you *can* invite them, don't you, Eddie? If you want to.' Yet in spite of this I didn't. Nor, for that matter, did I go to have tea with them very often; and when I did, it was usually close to Christmas when there would be other children present.

'Come along, Edwin,' I can hear their mothers say, in that slightly singsong way of speaking that mothers of small children often use, as they encouraged me to join in some party game such as 'Pass the Thimble', or 'Comes a Daddy Workman Looking for a Job' – a game that I detested, since it involved having to mime being the workman and whatever job he might be in search of.

They were painful times for me. I never felt as if I belonged to that world of other children – and, as I have suggested before, my real life lay more in my imagination, and in my being alone; on my Saturday walks, for instance, to my aunt and uncle's farm. That was the very centre of my life just then. Not at home: not in my parents' house; but free in the countryside, relating to the animals and the fields.

One very strange perspective was given to me when I went to my father's funeral, and found myself such a stranger to most of those at the service – quite a few of them local people, farmers, etc. – who had known my parents in recent years, but didn't know me – although they had heard of me, of course.

For as the hymns were being sung and as the prayers were being said, and as the words 'Man that is born of woman hath but a short time to live' rang out with such sonority, reminding everyone there of their mortality, I saw them glance at me from time to time and it made me nervous. For, in a way, I did feel slightly ashamed of myself – ashamed to have been my parents' only child, yet to be finding myself such a stranger there among them. However, there was nothing to be done, I remember telling myself as I felt my aunt, who was standing beside me, touch my elbow in sympathy. What had happened couldn't be unpicked – couldn't be undone.

Fortunately, it was only my aunt and uncle and Amy who came back to the house after the funeral was over. We had tea, and that was difficult enough, although we did manage to recall certain things with affection – particularly my mother's laugh. We even enjoyed a joke or two from Amy about my father's gambling habits, and how she would often be called upon to place bets for him on the horses. But it didn't go on for long, because I think that they were all aware of the confusion in me, and knew that there was no way of making things any different or any better.

The surprise of that day, however, was when Amy, who had stayed on at the house to get supper, suddenly announced to me, after my aunt and uncle had left, that her son, Tom, and her husband, Bill, were going to call to collect her later, and that they wanted us all to go to the Castle Inn for a drink.

That really startled me. For although I had had that intimate relationship with Tom when I was young (a relationship that had continued for quite a while, by the way – in fact, for almost a year) I don't think that I had ever spent any time with Amy's husband. I did know him – obviously – because he would sometimes call at the house to see Amy; and just once, I remember how I had gone to their house for some reason and he had been there. So to be suddenly going to have a drink with the three of them seemed strange; and I told Amy so.

'Strange?' she said. 'What's strange about it? We're all fond of you. We always were. And besides, Eddie, you need cheering up, so a drink would do you no harm.'

Which is how I found myself crossing the town's square later that evening, in the company of Amy and her two 'men', as she spoke of them – and all four of us going into the Castle Inn's 'Snuggery', as it was called, a small room beyond the main bar, in which a seat with a tall back – a wooden settle, that is – formed a half-circle facing the fire.

Tom insisted on buying the drinks – or the first round, at least – and despite protests from me, went off to order them, as Amy and I and her husband made ourselves comfortable.

Apart from us, there was only a young couple in the room, who sat watching the fire in silence, which we found a little inhibiting. But once Tom had returned, bearing the drinks upon a small tray with the word 'Worthington' painted upon it – the name of a brand of beer – we immediately began to relax.

'Good to see you, Eddie,' said Amy's husband, lifting his glass to me. 'Spitting image of his father, though,' he said to his wife, which I knew to be true, but which no longer really bothered me.

'In looks only, I hope,' Amy added with a smile.

And we sat there, the four of us, literally passing the time like that for almost two hours. I can't for the life of me remember what we talked about. I just recall the feeling of relief it gave me to have Tom seated beside me, and to have him recreating through silence the brief bond that we had enjoyed when we were young. And to have Amy and her husband making me feel that I did really belong to them in some way: that I had grown up with them and that I was close to them as a result.

At one moment Amy insisted that she be allowed to buy a round of drinks herself; and in order to avoid her husband preventing her from doing so, pressed a note into my hand and asked me to do it for her.

'Go on, Eddie,' she said. 'Please. Take no notice of *them*; of those two. They don't think women should *be* out drinking, let alone buying a round. But I love to go out, and to pay if I can. It does me good.'

I so appreciated it all: the warmth of their company; the good humour of our exchange; the red, shiny faces, brought on by the heat of the fire, combined with the alcohol we had consumed; and I did feel genuinely happy for once as we re-crossed the square to Tom's car before saying goodbye.

'Come and see us soon,' Amy half whispered to me as I kissed her; and Tom said something similar as he shook my hand.

'Goodnight all,' a man who had been crossing the square behind us called out; to which we all responded in chorus, bidding him goodnight in return – even though I quickly gathered from Amy that neither she nor Tom nor her husband had any idea who the well-wisher might have been.

'Sleep well,' were Amy's last words to me, and I remember that I did: that as I let myself into the house, knowing that I was going to spend the night there alone, I felt that some important change had taken place; that some chapter of my life had closed and that a new one was about to begin. And which is exactly what did happen, as this notebook of mine reveals.

Do notebooks go on and on, though? I am beginning to wonder. I can imagine that a diary might, if it is of a daily or of a weekly kind, and that one could keep such a thing for ever, as a kind of companion to one's life. But a notebook? Isn't that just a short-lived thing?

Something written out of a particular need – perhaps to clear something up; to create a sense of order? If it is, then the thing to do, I guess, is to go on writing it until there's no need to do so any longer; or until it changes into something else – something different. What I do know is that these thoughts have been a great help to me; that although I don't write them down regularly, or very often (there have been times when several weeks have gone by before I've felt the need to pick up my pen), I have got to know myself better, both through them and because of them: that they have enabled me to look into myself and to see myself more clearly. But what – or, rather, *who* – I don't see clearly or very objectively is Mark, I am afraid. I've mentioned him a lot because he has come to play quite a big part in my life, but I don't think that anyone reading these notes will have been given much of a picture of him.

So perhaps I must attempt to put that right and to say something here about that person who is now so dear to me, and who (Mark and I have talked about this) could even become a kind of life-partner of mine – if I don't muck it up, that is, which I still fear is what I am likely to do.

So, this morning, when we were still in bed, I told Mark that I am going to attempt to paint his portrait. He thought I meant paint it in paint, not words; then said he didn't know why I wanted to do such a thing, and was sure I wouldn't be good at it, which annoyed me a little.

'Why?' I asked him.

'Why what? Why wouldn't you be good at it?'

'Yes, why?'

'Because you're not observant, Eddie – that's why. Or not enough.'

'How do you *mean*?' I answered, surprised by this.

'Well: take my eyes, for instance. Tell me what colour they are. Right now. Without looking at them, I mean . . . Go on – say. Tell me.'

'Well – they're a –'

'There you are, you see,' said Mark, cutting in. 'You don't know. As I said, you're not very observant: not with regard to details, at least. How tall am I?'

'Well – you're *over* six feet.'

'Yes, but how *much* over?'

'Two inches,' I guessed.

'Three,' he answered. 'And weight?' he asked. 'How heavy am I?'

'That I don't know. You've never told me. You're heavier than I am, though, so somewhere around twelve stone, I guess.'

'And what else do you know?'

'What else? Well, I know that you have a sister. You've spoken about her. Emily, she's called – isn't she? And one brother – or is it two? – and you are the eldest.'

'Yes. And –?'

'And – well, that I like you a lot: that you're the first person I've grown to really like. The first friend, I mean. I like my aunt and uncle, of course – love them, in fact; and Amy too. You've heard me speak about Amy, haven't you, Mark? She was my parents' –'

'Yes, yes,' Mark answered impatiently. 'And Tom? What about him?'

'Well, yes, I liked him – yes, I did. But it was just a childhood thing – or more a *teenage* one, really, since Tom was older.'

'And what about *my* parents, Eddie? I know a lot about yours. What about mine?'

'Well, I know they are both alive and are together

– you've told me that – but not altogether happy. Is that right?'

'Correct,' said Mark, who by now seemed to be almost cross-examining me.

'And marks?' he asked.

'Marks? How do you mean?'

'On my body. Any marks? Anything unusual – notice-able?'

'Oh – *that!*' I said with a laugh, thinking of the large brown mole on one of his thighs.

'Well – that's a part of me, isn't it?' he said, suddenly sitting up and turning to face me. 'If it's to be a detailed portrait you're going to paint. . . . And what about tem-perament, then? Am I difficult? Easy to get on with? Selfish? Or what?'

I paused before replying to this because to do so wasn't easy.

'Quite selfish, at *times*,' I then said carefully. 'Yes. You are. Definitely. You certainly know your own mind, and you certainly like to have your own way; over lots of things.'

'But not over everything.'

'No – of course not. In any case, I'm such a ditherer that that side of your character tends to appeal to me. It's something I enjoy.'

'Am I a drinker, would you say? A boozer?' was his next question.

'You like a drink. Quite a few, in fact. But no, you're not a real drinker – far from it; any more than I am one myself.'

'And a smoker?'

'No – though I have seen you smoke a *cigar*.'

'But not a pipe.'

'No.'

'Never?'

'Never.'

'Well. Never trust a man who smokes a pipe, Eddie, is my advice to you,' he said with a smile. 'So – can you trust me, do you think?'

'Yes. I *think* so. In fact, I *know* so.'

'And what about deeper things?' he continued. 'Is this chap Mark, who runs a wine-bar in Fulham, who is taller than you are – heavier than you are – has two brothers and a sister – a loving person, would you say? Or not?'

'In my experience, yes,' I answered. 'Definitely. In fact, I think –'

'Yes?'

'I think that I'm in love with him. That we love one another.'

This was the first time that I had said this to Mark, although he had questioned me often enough about my feelings.

'Well, that's about it, then – isn't it?' Mark replied, pretending not to have heard what I had just said. 'Enough for a portrait, I think – don't you?' he added – much as I could see that he was pleased.

'Oh – and he *paints*, Eddie,' Mark added as a tease. 'Not *writes*, Eddie. *Paints*. Badly.'

'Not *that* badly, Mark.'

'Not as good as Piero, though,' he added. At which we both laughed.

'Nor Stubbs. Nor Titian,' I said, as Mark got out of bed and slipped into his underpants and then went off into the bathroom, with the image fixing itself in my mind of his sturdy, well-built frame, his dark, slightly curly head of hair, and the small spray of finer hair that appeared as a smudge at the base of his spine.

'Oh, and how about my shoe-size, Eddie?' Mark asked jokingly as he returned.

'Twelve,' I said.

'Spot on,' he replied. 'Big feet, big something else, is what they say, isn't it?'

'As if *I* should know,' I answered, as I too slipped out of bed and began to dress. 'You know, Mark,' I said to him, 'one day, I'm going to do this to *you*.'

'Do *what*?' Mark asked, miming surprise and fear.

'Ask *you* a whole list of questions about *me* — that's what.'

'Oh, good . . . Well, there'll be no end to that — will there, Eddie?' he teased. '*Far* too complicated, *you* are. It'd take a whole *book* to paint a decent portrait of *you* . . . I'll tell you what, though: you have very nice skin and very nice eyes.'

'Do I?' I answered.

'Yes — you do,' he said, showing me that he meant it.

'And what colour are they?' I asked.

'Your eyes? Grey-green,' he replied snappily; and that is what they are.

A week ago there were no leaves on the trees as Mark and I were driving down to the West Country for our second visit together. The furrowed fields were dark — almost black: tidy, clean, ready for their winter pause — their time of fallowness.

'Can I read you a poem?' I said to Mark that evening, when we were changing in our room, with a fire burning in the grate and the curtains partly drawn.

'If you want to — yes,' Mark answered, not showing much interest. 'What poem is it?'

'One I've written myself,' I said. 'It's about winter.'

'Oh, go on then,' he said, combing his hair and looking at my reflection in the mirror.

So I read him this poem, which I had written previous week. It's not a very good one, but since to have written it was such a rare thing for me to have done, I wanted to share it.

> Deep into the earth I go,
> Into the dark soil where the seedlings grow;
> Above there might be ice and snow —
> And death if they too quickly show their heads.
> But not for me. No death for me.
> No sun shall find me easily and draw me up before
>   my time.

'Hey, Eddie! That's not bad,' was Mark's reaction. 'Very *you*, as well. Always holding yourself back — aren't you? — in the shade. Not wanting to be drawn out. Not wanting to have your secrets discovered.'

'But I'm less like that now than I *was*, Mark,' I replied. 'A lot less secretive now. More ready to share than I was.'

'Of course you are,' Mark answered warmly, sensing quickly that he might have been hurtful. 'Of course you are, Eddie. A lot. We've both changed, that's the truth of the matter. That's what we're meant to do. Learn and grow — together.'

'If we can,' I said.

'Yes — well, if we can,' he added wisely.

Later, as we were on our way to bed, Mark returned to the subject of my secrecy and introversion; and this provoked a slight quarrel between us, because I thought that what had at first seemed a light tease had become something more akin to a taunt.

'But, Mark! We talked about that earlier,' I protested. 'I told you. I'm just made that way. I just am.'

'Yes, but it would be better if you weren't,' he said. 'Think what you're missing.'

'What I'm *missing*?' I asked.

'Yes. You live in a dream world, Eddie. In fact, I

sometimes wonder what you've been up to all these years.'

'All *what* years?' I almost snapped back at him.

'Well, all the years before we met. You don't realise it, but you never talk about them. You speak about when you left home and about your first years in London, when you lived with those two weird blokes in Battersea; but never about the years between – between then and now.'

'I *do*,' I protested. 'I'm *sure* I do.'

'You don't, Edwin,' said Mark emphatically. 'All I know is that you left Battersea to move to Chelsea – to where you live now; and that's about it.'

I quickly thought about this, wondering if it was really true; then realised that to some extent it was. For I had never spoken to Mark about Patrick, for example; nor had I ever said very much about the work that I did or about the colleagues at my office; although the reason for the latter was simply that it was such plodding, tedious work, in which I took little interest.

'I mean, you must have had friends during those years,' said Mark. 'You must have had affairs – had lovers.'

And strangely enough, I felt too ashamed to be able to tell him that I hadn't; that I had been forced to seek sexual relief occasionally with some stranger, but during that time had formed no real relationship; only Patrick, Len and Thelma had been my friends. It seemed that the deaths of my parents, followed so quickly as they had been by the arrival of Mark in my life, had acted as some kind of turning-point that had lifted me out of myself. So all I said to Mark in reply was, 'Well, I had a few affairs, Mark. Of course I did. But they weren't very interesting. None of them are worth talking about.'

'Oh, Eddie – you are an odd one,' Mark answered with a laugh, suddenly pushing me through the doorway of our room and on to our bed. 'You know,' he said, 'there are a lot of things going on out there, in that big, wide world of ours . . . This year, a man walked on the moon, for instance. And a woman – yes, a woman, Eddie – was made the prime minister of Israel. These things count, you know.'

'And Judy Garland died,' I said, a little wickedly.

'Judy who?'

'Garland. She died.'

'Well, there you are,' he answered, giving me a quick shake that soon turned into a hug. 'At least you are aware of *something* that's gone on outside that little dream world of yours . . . Come on, Eddie. Let's turn in. Put out the lights and go to bed.'

To which I readily agreed, knowing that Mark and I would be lying there in silence for a while, inhaling the apple sweetness of the air that wafted about the room and scented everything in it. Not strongly, but with a very pale, very delicate perfume.

XII

TODAY THERE'S BEEN such big news! Thelma announced that she's found a job for herself – a full-time one; and doing exactly what she's been wanting to do, which is to run – she said 'manage' – a restaurant.

She announced this when she and Len and I were having Sunday lunch together (Mark not being there because of his work) – saying she had something to tell us that she thought we ought to know. And I have to admit that both Len and I were quite stunned by the news.

'But *where*, Thelma?' was Len's first response. 'And *how*?'

'South Kensington. A bistro,' she said. 'Saw it in the *Standard*. In the ads.'

'And actually *running* it? Actually managing it?' Len went on, a little too questioningly, I thought.

'Yes,' Thelma answered. 'Of course.'

'How do you mean – "of course", Thelma? You've never *done* such a thing: never *had* such a job.'

'I know. But I do know a hell of a lot about it – don't I? Through you. I've listened to all your worries and troubles for years, Len. Helped you to sort them out. Discussed changes, plans – different menus and so on – so I'm not exactly a novice, am I?'

'No. But –'

'I think Len is surprised, Thelma. That's all it is, isn't

it, Len?' I said, cutting in, wanting to relax the feeling of tension there was between them. 'Isn't that so, Len? She's been pretty secretive about it, though – hasn't she? You *have*, you know, Thelma.'

'Well, what if I have?' Thelma replied, with a quick toss of her head. 'You don't get anywhere if you talk too much. Deeds count more than words.'

'Well then,' said Len, puffing out his cheeks a little and obviously adjusting to the idea. 'We've got to – well, congratulate you, haven't we? Haven't we, Eddie? . . . An extra glass of wine is what is called for here, I think. Come on. Let me top that one up for you, Eddie; and let's drink to – well, to Thelma, shall we? The new manageress.'

As Len and I lifted our glasses and wished Thelma well, I saw how deeply nervous Thelma had been made by this sudden new direction her life had taken.

'Are we allowed to kiss her?' Len said jokingly. 'Or do we just shake hands?'

A strong blush began to colour Thelma's cheeks, and the three of us then clung together and kissed each other and laughed.

I am now thirty-three years old, and all my adult life I have struggled to free myself from my past; yet I've done so only a little, it seems to me. But perhaps it will always be like that. Perhaps to be really free of it wouldn't be right – be good. That's what I'm having to learn, it seems. For as I have made these mental trips into times gone by, I see that what is there, lying behind me, is not really there at all; not trapped in time as I think it is. Instead, it is free and alive and playing its part in making me what I am – what I have become. The wheel keeps turning. The understandings change from day to day. I remember how Patrick said to me once – Patrick, the Irishman, I mean, who used to be my neighbour. 'You'll never pin it down, Eddie,' he said. 'You can't nail time. It's ever on the move. Ever on the go.'

He said that one night after we had slept together for the first time, when I had been restless, feeling guilty about being with him on account of my age.

'Oh, Jesus, Eddie,' he said. 'What's wrong with us enjoying ourselves, for Christ's sake? Kiss the joy as it flies, lad – that's what you need to do. Life's short. You know that – don't you? It's here and gone in no time. You won't be thinking that right now, when you're so young, but you'll know it as you grow older. Look. You like me – don't you? You enjoy being with me. You enjoy it when I kiss you in the way that I do – when I make you relax; when I ease you into it. And there's a shiny new moon up there in the heavens tonight, sending its blessings down. So what more do you want for us than that?'

I loved to hear Patrick speak in that way – the soft, lilting sounds of his voice would always enchant me.

'Thinking of your dad, are you?' he would sometimes ask, when there were signs of my being morose. 'Is that what it is? . . . Well, I'll tell you what, Eddie, he wasn't thinking of you – was he? – when he treated you the way he did. Kiss it as it flies, Eddie. Let go. Give in . . .'

'Hey – look,' he once said to me, as he turned on to his back naked, in order to display his lanky body. 'How about this, then? With its John Thomas all erect and all the saints of Ireland looking down at it in amazement. For there's not many will have seen the likes of that, Eddie – I can tell you.'

And I knew that he was right: that it is wrong to be so retentive, in the way that I tend to be. 'Come here,' he said, pulling me close to him and drawing me into his arms. 'You're a lovely boy, you are. Do you know that? What do I have to do to make you happy?'

I had no answer to that. For I was then just seventeen years old, and knew myself much less well than I do today. All I could say to him in reply was that I was grateful for what he had done for me; for waking me up to things that I needed to know and that I really ought to have known by then. And for the short time that we were together I did know, I did experience, a happiness of sorts. He didn't have the steadiness of character that Mark seems to be blessed with. He was more mercurial – and always looking for change. But when he gave, he gave – totally; with no barriers, no conditions.

'Jesus,' he said one day, after we had known each other for some time. 'You're an odd chappie, you are, you know. But you're going to meet someone someday who'll get the hang of you better than I can' – which, when I look back at it, seems to have been a prediction that looked ahead to my first meeting with Mark, which had been in that bar in Piccadilly. That same bar to which I had first been taken by Patrick when he had been showing me the town, and when, on the top deck of a bus coming home, we had encountered that noisy band of boisterous women.

The year is now drawing to a close, with the days shorter, the nights colder and much longer, and with a touch of frost in the early hours before the day begins. Somewhere, a long way off, tucked into the folds of the Exmoor hills, is the small town in which I was born, and to which, after so many years of being away from it, I have only recently returned. Now, with the winter drawing near, things there will be peaceful for a while, as the countryside draws itself together for the festival of Christ's birth; after which there will be the frosts and snows that mark the beginning of the year before the sudden advent of a new spring; later to be followed by the fulfilment of a new summer.

Little by little. Day by day. What was it some wise sage once said – some Greek, I think – that the beautiful comes about through many numbers? Well, I don't know that much about beauty. My life has been too curbed, too restricted, for me to grasp the full meaning of that word. Mark grumbles because I'm not 'open' enough – always being so watchful, he says, so very careful, and always ready to see the negative side of things. But I do have some idea of what beauty might be, and occasionally, in some odd moment when I'm caught out (which is usually when I'm not thinking too much), I catch a glimpse of something that might be it: seeing everything not in a golden light exactly, but certainly in a different and more optimistic one than is my general view of the world.

What an odd thing memory is, though. The way it works. How almost anything can trigger it into action. I experienced this yet again today, after returning home from work; when, for some reason – I am not sure what – an image suddenly surfaced out of the past and came floating into my mind: of one of the labourers who worked on my uncle's farm, a man that I saw regularly as a child, when there on my weekly visits. A swarthy, not very attractive character, with a hooked nose and beady, glittering eyes – the memory of him is a haunting one.

Rusty is what he was called, I think, or what he was known as, rather, since it was obviously some kind of nick-name. And I suddenly recalled how his eyes would often watch me from within the shadow of some barn, or from the corner of a haystack in the fields, as I was going about doing the little jobs I had been set to do – collecting eggs from the chicken runs; or apples, perhaps, that had fallen before their time, but that my aunt would none the less use for making chutney. And I knew that I was afraid of him.

Not that he was ever rude to me; nor did he ever show signs of there being anything violent in his nature. But young though I was, I sensed a need to be careful and not to engage with him at all – although now, as I look back, I cannot think why.

What did he see in me, I wonder? What was he projecting on to me – or on to my image, rather? His own youth, perhaps? Some aspect of consciousness? I really don't know. Or did it have to do with a loss of innocence, I wonder – that, by using me as some kind of object for his projection, he was seeking to recover?

Whatever, he was an unusual figure – one deeply bound up with the natural world of the countryside, the world in which he grew up and in which he had always lived. For people used to say of him (it was my uncle who told me this) that he was capable of wizardry, and of casting some curious kind of spell. That there were times when he had been seen alone, at dusk, in the corner of a meadow – where, as the light began to fade, he could be heard making a peculiar kind of whistling noise that attracted small animals to him – wild animals, I mean; so that, as darkness fell, he could be seen surrounded by stoats, weasels, hedgehogs and the like; occasionally, it was said, even by a badger or a fox.

He sometimes slept in the open too, and on hot summer nights could be seen bedding himself down beneath some hedgerow, where he would slumber until dawn.

He didn't look like an Englishman – more like a Spaniard or an Italian; with locks of jet-black hair that pushed themselves out from beneath the grey tweed cap he always wore; and with slightly sallow, oily skin – and (I recall how this used to disturb me) very wet, red lips and a tendency to dribble.

He drank a lot as well. Mostly cider – very rough farm cider, that in winter he would drink hot: heated, as I recall, in a pointed copper cone that had been thrust into the fire.

'You wants to see a little frog being swallowed alive?' he would say to visitors to the area, whom he might meet in the local bars when scrounging money or a drink from them. At which they would usually laugh

– until, to their astonishment, he produced a live frog from his pocket.

'Now,' he would say, 'do you want to see 'im going down legs first or head first?' To which when asked what the difference would be, he replied, 'If 'ee goes down head first, you'll see 'im kickin' for joy. If 'ee goes down legs first, you'll see the look of 'orror in 'ee's eyes.'

One day – it must have been when I was in my early teens – this man Rusty called at my parents' house; and this being an unusual thing to have happened, my memory of it is a vivid one.

I recall that I was ill and in bed, suffering from some nasty form of bronchial flu. Also, that it was a Thursday, which meant that it was market-day and that both my parents were out.

I remember too that Amy was with me in the house and that it was she who answered the doorbell when it rang: a rather loud ring; and one that, after a pause of just a few seconds, was repeated.

Then I heard the sound of Amy's voice, and in reply to it, a voice I didn't recognise, although there did seem to be something familiar about its tones and rhythms.

I couldn't hear what words were being said because, although the door had been left ajar, my bedroom was tucked away at the very back of the house, above my father's study. None the less, I was able to guess from the verbal pattern of the exchange that Amy had let someone in and had closed the door behind them.

Being curious to know who the visitor might be, I listened carefully, and after a pause heard the sound of footsteps on the stairs, accompanied by the sound of Amy's voice, issuing some kind of instruction.

'Top floor,' was all I could hear, followed by, 'The door will be open.'

The footsteps then continued; and, before long, there was a knock on my bedroom door.

'Yes?' I called out, now anxious to know who it could be, and thinking to myself that it couldn't be Tom, since he had been to see me only the day before, and in any case he wouldn't be needing directions regarding the whereabouts of my room.

So it was really to my very great astonishment that I saw the face of Rusty appearing in front of me, and disturbingly close to me as well.

'Can I come in?' he asked, in his coarse, West Country voice.

'Oh, yes, do,' I replied, rapidly sitting up in bed. 'Do . . . please.'

He had removed the peaked cloth cap he always wore when out of doors, and I remember how this had changed his image in a rather striking fashion, making him appear much younger than I had imagined him to be from my somewhat distant encounters with him on the farm. And I had never thought that he could smile, as he did then; nor that the jet-black locks of his hair, which always thrust themselves out so wildly from beneath the edges of his cap, would be as long as they were, so that as he pushed them away from his forehead they clung together, seeming almost to pin themselves back; drawing themselves towards the nape of his neck, and making him look, I thought, rather like some rough, eighteenth-century seaman.

What was also very striking, now that he was close to me, and caught, as he was, in a sharp shaft of light that struck across the room from its one tall window, was that the colour of his skin, which, on the farm, had always seemed to be a kind of brownish-grey or olive, broken only by the savage scarlet of his lips, now seemed a near russet-gold.

'I've brought this for you,' he said, holding out a large

cone of newspaper, in which, as if it might have been a bouquet of roses, there was an enormous bunch of dark-green watercress; the leaves of which sparkled with tiny drops of dew.

'I've just picked it for you, Edwin,' he said. 'From the river bank . . . Your aunt told me you liked it. She said it would cheer you up: make you feel better.'

I hardly knew how to reply to this – how to thank him. His physical presence – his closeness – the intensity of his gaze as he handed me his gift, made me feel shy of him.

'You do like it – don't you?' he asked, with a look of deep puzzlement in his eyes. 'The cress,' he said. 'You do like it?'

'Oh, yes – I do!' I blurted out, now taking his offering but still not thanking him for it.

'Well, I hope you'll be better soon, young man,' he answered, with a quick, clumsy nod of his head. 'You didn't mind – did you? – my coming to see you?'

'Oh, of course not,' I stuttered in reply. 'It's really kind of you. Really thoughtful' – spoken, I hoped, with at least the semblance of a smile.

He looked at me intently for a while, as if he might have been fixing a picture of me in his mind, then glanced swiftly about the room, taking in the dark Victorian furniture, the large china washbasin, with its matching, rose-patterned jug, the wardrobe, with its large bevel-edged mirrors, in which, I realised, he could see a reflection of me in my bed.

His eyes paused for a few seconds before moving on to the bed itself, then back from it to me.

'Shall I ask Mrs Gibson to put the cress in water?' he asked. 'Take it down with me?'

'Well, yes – perhaps,' I replied. 'Thank you. That would be nice.'

'They were born in it, you see,' he said, 'in water, and can't be parted from it for long.'

He rubbed his right hand against the rough tweed jacket he was wearing and held it out to me; but I, behaving stupidly, chose not to take hold of it, as if I had failed to understand the gesture he was making.

'Shake hands – shall we?' he asked. 'Make everything better?'

Writing about it now, I can hardly believe that this event took place. To me, it seems that it happened in some dream: that this golden, russet-faced man had stepped into my room from some unknown place in time, in order to exchange those few, brief words with me before slipping on his cap again and exiting through the door. Yet that night, when Amy came to my room to see how I was, I remember how she brought with her a plateful of delicious watercress sandwiches. And I am quite sure that they were real, and not of some other place and time, because I am able to recall with such precision their various tastes and textures: the soft, spongy white of the freshly baked bread; the creamy yellow of the lightly salted butter that had been spread upon it with such care; and then, pressed into the centre of the sandwiches, the sharp, bitter, peppery taste of the watercress itself.

Oddly – just to show how the unconscious handles and works with experience – I didn't mention this visit to either of my parents, and as nothing was ever said to me about it by them, I don't think that Amy did, either.

When I next saw my aunt, I did manage to thank her and to say to her what a kind thought the present of cress had been. But I said nothing about the bearer of the gift: about how surprised – indeed, how startled – I had been to have had him call at our house without warning. And all my aunt said to me in reply was, 'Well, you've always been fond of watercress, haven't you, Eddie? From when you were small. Always a little odd you were in that respect, because it's not something children tend to like.'

So the presence close to me of that dark yet gilded figure remains protected from exposure, trapped in some odd capsule of my mind; as if it belongs to my inner life more than to my outer one – as, indeed, do so many memories, it would seem: acting, perhaps, as fodder for the life we live underneath; for that vein of rich, unfolding narrative within us.

Perhaps (I don't know what makes me want to write this) the appearance of this figure in my room had been a sign, a pointer, of some change that was taking place. For looking back at it, it seems to me that, out of the shadow he had always stood for in my mind, something within the orbit of my psychic world had transformed itself into gold, and Rusty's arrival, which had so startled me, was connected with some alchemy of the spirit. The 'whites' of that gold – its precipitate – being the sparkle of the dewdrops on the gift he had brought, set against the dark green of the wild watercress.

Well – there they are: so many forgotten things that have been stored away. What a repository of them there seems to be in the mind. I can't write of them all; for if I did, then I would never release myself from this journal of mine, which I have noticed of late is something that I am now beginning to want to do. After all, I am not a real writer – not a professional one. I just scrawl and scribble away and am far too slapdash to be that. And, as Mark said to me once, after he had glanced at a few pages I had set down (ones that said nothing about my secret 'collection', of course), it would be quite difficult to decipher much of what I have written. 'Take a clever old stick to sort that lot out,' he said.

However, I have enjoyed it – that's the important thing;

and it has certainly helped me through a difficult time; through such a big turning-point in my life. The old and the new; the present and the past – all mixing; all blending; all making up the web of life; all weaving its new fabric. And yet, this journal's still not done, I think. Whatever the purpose of it has been, it's still not finished.

Am I happy? Well, I tend to avoid that word, because experience has taught me that the shadows in me can return at any moment. But I know that I am certainly a great deal more pleased with myself than I was a year ago: am even in love, perhaps – something I never thought I could be; and I count that quite an achievement. Whether or not I shall be able to maintain my relationship with Mark, I have no idea; but I say to myself (always, I have to confess, with a slight feeling of pain) that it's wisest not to think in that way. Just live for now, I say – for the present. Just be glad to be here – where I am, *how* I am; in this flat; in London; close to the river. For me, that is – that *has* to be – enough.

Such a dream I had last night! I felt compelled to jot it down at once, before I got up, before it got swallowed up by time.

I was alone – in a room. Naked, I think – for although I couldn't see myself at all, I certainly felt as if I had no clothes on – and I was sitting facing a blue-grey wall that I thought was made of stone.

For some reason, I appeared to be hypnotised by this wall and just sat there staring at it. Then, gradually, its blue-grey colours began to shift and change: small particles of brown and black beginning to appear among them, quickly followed by sudden streaks and flashes of white.

I then realised that the wall wasn't a solid wall at all, but was composed of these constantly moving fragments – and for a moment or two I felt strangely cold, and wanted to draw something around me. But I was unable to do so because, as I said, I was naked and had no clothing with me. So I just sat there shivering – all the while looking at (now more looking *into*) this wall.

The atmosphere in the room became intense, and I somehow knew that if I kept on staring at the wall it would surrender something to me: that (as if emerging from a mist) something would appear through it, or out of it. What it would be, I couldn't imagine, but I knew that the thought of it made me nervous.

Then, as if from a long way off, I heard a voice calling my name. 'Edwin,' it called out – not 'Eddie'; which it then repeated several times.

I thought that the voice might be that of my father, and that this was why I felt so nervous. Then, very slowly, my father's features began to appear in front of me, emerging from the ever-shifting fragments out of which the wall appeared to be composed.

At first, I could tell only vaguely that it was him, but gradually the image began to strengthen; its shapes, forms, colours grew more definite – until it finally settled and became almost static. Not entirely so. I was aware that it too was composed of fragments, and that like the wall in which it had been contained, and out of which it had just emerged, there was continual movement within it.

Nonetheless, there, immediately in front of me, was a pretty definite image of my father, who was looking directly at me. I could clearly make out the neat cut of his hair, with its streaks and patches of grey close to the temples; and the familiar cool, grey-green of his eyes, with their curious overlay of gold, that now, in the half-light (for it seemed that the room contained no windows of any kind, and by some means or another lit itself from within), gleamed and glinted as they looked across at me – seeming almost to study me.

At first, I felt so overcome by this sight that I was

tempted to look away; but I recall telling myself (all this was in the dream) that the moment was an important one; that I shouldn't seek to escape from it or avoid it. So, nervous though I was – I stared back. And as I did, my father turned his head to one side, allowing me to study it in profile.

And what so surprised me was the sudden sense of pride I felt: the sudden feeling of gladness that I was given, to know, as I did then, that this was my parent – the man who had fathered me, who begat me.

He was wearing one of the white, neatly cut shirts that he put on each morning after breakfast: the collar crossed by the edging of the grey-green cardigan he was wearing; the hair, where it touched the collar, just turning over it in a neat and orderly fashion.

Then I stood up, thinking that I would cross the room to get a closer view of my father's image. I was aware that it wasn't tangible – wasn't solid – and that it would be impossible for me to touch him, but I wanted to go nearer; to go closer to him; almost to join him in some way.

No sooner did that thought come to me, however, than the image turned away and began to move off, to dissolve and become part of the composition of the wall again, which made me sad. So sad in fact that as I again sat down upon my stool – or was it a chair? (what I was seated upon wasn't clear) – I saw a tear drop on to one of my hands, and felt its dampness upon my skin. And when I looked up, I found to my astonishment that my father's image had returned – the head now closer than before and nodding slowly up and down.

And then – oh, I hardly know how to write this! – my father smiled at me. It was a slow, very steady kind of smile; one that took a long time to form; but it was definitely that – definitely a smile, I mean.

'Father?' I called out. 'Can you hear me?' – to which he only nodded again in reply.

'Can you hear me?' I then repeated, hoping, I suppose, that he would speak to me. But he didn't – couldn't, perhaps; because, I thought to myself, we are existing in different times: ones that sounds are unable to bridge. But he went on nodding at me, as if to signify, I dared to think, that he was aware of what I was feeling.

Had he seen my tear, I wondered – that was so quickly followed by others? And was he now, almost two years after his death, asking me to forgive him for all the smiles that he had denied me over the years?

I would like to think that this was so. All I know is that, since waking this morning, I have experienced a sense of joy, of happiness, the like of which I have never known.

'What the *hell* are you doing?' Mark asked, having been wakened by the rustlings of my paper and the scratchings of my pen.

'I'm writing,' I said. 'Go back to sleep.'

'You and your bloody writing, Eddie,' Mark muttered. 'What the hell are you writing about now?'

'Just my dream, Mark,' I answered. 'Go back to sleep.'

'Your dream! What do you want to write about your bloody dream for?'

'Because I do, Mark – that's why. Go back to sleep now. It's only half-past five.'

'Half-past bloody five!' Mark protested, turning on to his side and drawing the bedclothes over him. I then read through the notes I had scribbled down, just to make sure that I had captured some of what had been offered to me in my sleep, the memory of which had made me happy.

XIII

TODAY BEING A Sunday, I would normally be having lunch with Len and Thelma; sometimes with Mark if he's not working; at others just the three of us – just Len, Thelma and myself. All that has changed, however, because Thelma's 'bistro', as she insists upon calling it, is open – and she has to be there.

Mark and I called to see her during the week to see how she was getting on, and she greeted us in such a professional way. Warmly, of course, but not in a particularly personal manner – showing us to a table and handing us a menu.

'If you're expecting special attention, you're not getting it,' she said with a quick laugh as she bounced away and sent a waiter to take our order.

I was really impressed by her. Mark was, too. She seemed so at home, so good at what she was doing; it was as if she had been doing it all her life. And I really am so pleased for her. She seemed almost a different person; as if, in some way, she had suddenly come into focus: had become more defined.

I'm not sure that Len is as pleased for her as I am; but perhaps that is because he enjoys routine; enjoys life's regular patterns; and here he is, having to struggle with a new one.

So, with Thelma at work, doing what she wanted to do; and with Mark and I still pleased with each other and with the daily deepening of our relationship, for once my life and the life around me seems orderly and full of promise. Having said that, however, there is one thing that bothers me – that goes on bothering me; appearing at times to be almost threatening me in some way – which has to do with the lumber room (as I call it) in my flat, which still remains a secret as far as its contents are concerned; in that no one – not even Mark – is aware of them.

For I find that if I happen to think of that room it creates quite a tension in my mind, in that I then find myself wanting to do something about it – to take action: perhaps dispose of all my trophies, as I think of them – give them away to someone – *anyone* – clear the decks, so to speak, and put them into the past; into a life that I used to lead but that I am now leading no longer. The fact being that for quite some time now I've not stolen anything at *all* – not even a box of matches, which, in the past, used to be a convenient way of relieving myself when the compulsion from which I suffer began to take hold of me and possess me.

I cannot say that I am cured. It would be rash of me to do that, because the mind is such a tricky thing and so easily creates illusions. But I do feel as if I am almost free of it. As if, at last, after so many years, I am well on the way to being cured.

Could it be that the healing power of having Mark in my life has effected this? Or has it to do with my parents' deaths, and the distance I have now gained from them both, which allows me to view them differently – particularly my father? Could it also be because I have gone back into the past, returning to what used to be my home: to the house in which I was born and to all that I ran away from?

The answer is, I guess, that it is a mixture of all these things. Outwardly, alas, a reconciliation with my father proved impossible, much as I believe that I was ready for it – and, perhaps, wanted it. But inwardly, I feel that *something* of that kind has taken place. For if I think of my father now (as I happened to do this morning when I was shaving) I no longer feel angry with him, or afraid of him in the way that I used to do. On the contrary, I now feel for him an almost tender, muted affection: an affection that his spirit appeared to reciprocate when I saw his smiling image in my dream.

But about my things – my 'treasures'. About them – over them – hangs the question of whether I should expose them to someone or not. Say to Mark, perhaps, that they are there in that room – all stored away in their boxes. Tell him what they are, which is nothing less, of course, than a record of all my 'crimes'.

I do so wish that I was able to do that, and could get it over and done with. For if things between Mark and myself continue to develop positively, then he's bound to become inquisitive about what is kept there in that lumber room of mine.

'Why don't you clear it out, for heaven's sake,' he's going to say to me one day – and the idea of it upsets me; not a little, but a lot. Because I fear that this could become an issue between us. His wanting to have a good 'clear-out', as I can hear him calling it, and me not being able to give in; wanting to hold on to my secret for longer.

So, as the year draws towards its close, this is where I now am. Like the snail carrying its house upon its back, so I, it seems, must carry my lumber room on mine. And something tells me that I shall never be able to give it up; that, whatever happens, I shall always keep it – always guard it. Quite why, I don't know; but occasionally, if I am alone (or during the night, for instance, if I get out of bed to get a drink or to go to the lavatory), I sense that there might be something deep within me that is locked away in that room, and from which I gain, it would seem, some unusual form of security that I cannot gain elsewhere.

Perhaps, if I were to be open and honest about it with Mark, he would respect this need I have to maintain such an area of shadow. I doubt that he would understand it exactly, and would probably label me as being 'a bit bonkers' – a term he has used quite often in the past when he has learned of my various weaknesses. But at least he might respect my wishes regarding this, and, just out of a sense of decency towards me, might allow us to weave it into our life.

However, we've not come to that as yet. We don't even share a flat; don't even live together in that sense; and there is little danger of my having to expose this secret of mine unless he comes to settle here. So all that lies in the future – as do so many things. Right now, in the immediate future, is a trip to the National Gallery that I have planned for this afternoon. (Where better to go in London on a Sunday?) What shall I find there, I wonder? What shall I discover? The wondrous clarity of Gainsborough's painting of his two daughters? The creamy pinks and greys of a Turner seascape? Or will it be the precise mechanics of a Piero della Francesca – the painter Thelma had never heard of? His *Saint Michael*, perhaps; in which, as though in some way to distance himself from what he has just done, the rather boyish, muscular saint treads nonchalantly upon a serpent he has just slaughtered – the blood of which has left a delicate crimson smudge upon the cool-grey blade of his sword. And in which too, setting off in such a truly magical fashion the pale, almost chalky, colours that are so typical of this artist, there is the sharp intrusion of what at first appears to be black, but is, in fact, more of a deep cherry-red:

the narrow, curving shadow that lines the hem of the saint's tunic.

Whatever, it will be a great pleasure to be there – as it always is. Today, without Mark, unfortunately, because he has to be at work. However, I shall be able to speak to him about it on my return and I know he will enjoy that.

'As long as it's not bloody Rubens,' he'll say – because, hearty though Mark's general character might be, the slight coarseness of Rubens's work offends him. 'All tits and bums,' he says, 'that need pinching' – and at this I always laugh, because I find that expressive side of his character so endearing.

And perhaps (I have only just thought of this) it could be on such a jocular note as that that this journal of mine could end: for it has surely served its purpose. What might Amy be doing right now, I wonder? Clearing away the Sunday lunch things, I expect. And my aunt and uncle? Having a snooze, I dare say – their regular afternoon nap. And Rufus and Charlie? What might they be doing? Out walking the dogs? Doing the tango together? Or just listening to the radio?

As for my friend Len, I know what he'll be doing. With Thelma out at work he'll be lost in reading a book. At the moment, he's reading *The Desire and Pursuit of the Whole*, by Frederick Rolfe, a book that I enjoyed and a copy of which I have lent him. And Patrick, my Irish neighbour? Where might he be and what might he be doing? Smashing eggs? Making an omelette? Or out drinking in some bar? ('Propping up a Guinness', as he might put it.) And sensing, I hope, that I do think of him at times, and send him all my fondest thoughts and wishes.

As for Mark – well, I know where he is, don't I? At work in his wine-bar in Fulham; and tonight he will be here with me. Just two youngish men who enjoy each other a lot; and who, like so many other friends or other couples in this world, are nothing out of the ordinary. Aren't saints, or martyrs — aren't kings or politicians: just two souls among so many, whose lives are not very interesting from an exterior point of view, as this journal of mine has shown; but who little by little, day by day, help to create the basic fabric of life; weaving together the past and the present, the old and the new, to create from it the future.

Having decided when I came home last night that I had already brought this journal to a close, I am now about to put it away; my plan being to wrap it in some thick brown paper that I have discovered in a drawer, and then hide it with all my treasures.

I must confess that I am half tempted to destroy this book, because I know that what Mark said of it is true: that it would take a clever old stick to decipher much of my scrawl and scribble. But, who knows? Someone, some day, might take an interest in it. Who or how I have no idea; but there are a few bits of it at least — a few passages — that are worth reading.

It could be some writer, perhaps. They're always looking for copy — aren't they? I don't know any, unfortunately; but — well, at least it makes me not want to destroy what I have written.

Perhaps, eventually, I shall decide to give it to someone — someone I can trust. If not, then it will be here with me when I die; and then either Mark or Thelma or Len will take the decision for me.

So — here goes! Paper, string and a sticky label, saying what the parcel contains, will be enough; and then let its future be what it will be. Having written it, the best thing to do is to forget it, I think. I won't 'drown' my book, as Shakespeare's Prospero says he intends to do in *The Tempest*. I'll just consign it to what I shall think of as a temporary form of oblivion by hiding it in my lumber room with all the evidence of my misdeeds; and there upon it the dust of time can settle.

POSTSCRIPT

EDWIN CARPENTER DIED in 1990 at the age of fifty-four. According to Thelma Rillington, his relationship with his friend Mark had blossomed, and, because Edwin refused to move, they had lived together for quite a few years in Edwin's flat.

'Why it ended,' she said, 'I really don't know; but they were happy, I do know that – or certainly Edwin was. I didn't know then, of course, about Edwin's troubles.' (She meant his thieving.) 'I only learned about that after his death – from his writing, I mean. But I remember Mark saying to me one day that he had helped Edwin cure himself of a very bad habit, and how pleased he was about it. It was something he said only lightly, so I didn't take much notice of it. I thought, I suppose, that it was something small – something unimportant. Now, though, I know he meant the opposite, because I can still see the look in his eye as he said it.

'It's a pity Mark went out of Eddie's life,' she went on. 'A pity we can't contact him to let him know that Eddie has died. But perhaps he'll read the book,' she added with a laugh, 'and perhaps one day we'll get to hear *his* side of the story.'

When asked what she had done with Edwin's 'collection', which he had left her in his will, she smiled radiantly. 'Gave it all to charity,' she said, 'including the cash.' As if by doing this she had made a kind of offering for her friend; one that perhaps would serve for him as an act of absolution.